MADAME'S DOUBT
Paperback Edition
Copyright © 2013 by Keegan Lace

All rights reserved. No part of this book may be reproduced or transmitted in any form or by any means without written permission from the author.

ISBN ISBN-13: 978-1492813842
ISBN-10: 1492813842

Printed in USA by Bookista Publishing (www.bookistapublishing.com)

CHAPTER ONE

It was late morning and Victoria was deep in slumber beneath piles of linen sheets and goose down puffs. Heavy emerald velvet covered enormous windows to shield out the early spring sunshine. The sun was a tease at this time of year. Boots were beginning to dry from the winter rains and the lawn was ready to explode with fresh sprouts. The staff at the Markham Estate was busy preparing the equipment for spring sports. The moment before the bloom, the deluge reared its head again. This Saturday was a bonus day. A peak at the summer that all of Dover would welcome.

"Good morning my Lady. There you are love. Come. It is time to reveal yourself. Tea, before we prepare for repast with the man and your brother and sisters? Your Mother is half-way to London by now. She will be with her sister at Persimmon house. She is already preparing for June social season. Your father is about and out on horse. You will want to be ready upon his return."

Lady Victoria was in her seventeenth year. She was hopeful. Her world was getting larger as time passed and she had dreams of finding love like all girls of her age. She was sandwiched between an older brother and two younger sisters. Peter was 19, his military plans delayed due to sickness. Elaine was the baby at 15 and Mary was 16 years of age. Her mother was quick to have her children but for unknown reasons she stopped producing after Elaine. It left The Countess with time on her hands at an early age.

Countess Tompkins travelled to London in the springtime to assist her sister. Lady Sterling was preparing Persimmon House for the social season beginning in June. Peter met an appropriate girl in London the year prior and the marriage between the two was to be officially finalized. They had shared a lengthy courtship. The Honorable Jane Marley was a worthy match for Peter. She was 18 years old and guaranteed a healthy virgin. Peter would eventually inherit the entire Markham Estate and Jane was well suited to fill it with children. Victoria noticed a change come over her cherished brother with the mention of Jane. A delicate love born of mutual respect had blossomed between them. It gave Victoria hope that a similar love would fill her world someday.

"Lady Victoria. I sense the daydream in which you are lost. Time does not allow for it at this moment. Rush, you father will be waiting."

The Earl was a brutish sort to most who only briefly made his acquaintance. Victoria knew her father was a solitary man who loved his wife and children very much. He was actually a humorous gentleman, especially among his girls who were a constant source of amusement. He was like a cat in ways. Lady Victoria's father retained a sense of mystery and aloofness, but when treated in distinct manner by those close to him he was embraceable.

"I will be ready Esther. I want to roam the grounds in comfort today. Presentable yes, but something which allows for free movement."

Esther pulled out a light pink cotton dress with sky blue flowers and a velvet sash. It was high in the neck. She would go uncorseted. Her coltish figure did not require such impediments when not necessitated by custom. Victoria ran wild when allowed. With the Countess away in London and Father reading in his study, she would be free to do so. Esther had been with Lady Victoria since infancy. She was her maid, but so much more. Esther was a mother figure to Victoria, as her mother was busy with the younger girls. She shared and kept all of Victoria's privacies as she bolted through adolescence into young womanhood. Esther knew that matters between Peter and Jane were to be finalized but she was also aware that Victoria's betrothment was keen on her mother's mind. There was certainly something at hand. Powerless, she hoped for the best.

Victoria emerged from the washroom ready to be dressed for the day. Her alabaster skin showed a natural peach glow. Her sapphire eyes showed a good night's rest and a lack of years. She sat at the vanity to have her gossamer hair pulled back sensibly.

"My Lady, your golden locks look as though you have just emerged from a gale. I dare not imagine your dreams as you toss and turn so much. Your night cap is always discarded next to your bed by morning." Esther tamed her hair with a pearl handled hairbrush.

"Esther. Please, gentle. My tender scalp." Victoria fussed until Esther laid down the paddle. She stepped into her dress and fussed a bit more. A quick glance in the head to toe mirror tilted to welcome her presence and led to a nod. "Perfect as always Esther. I love you."

Victoria ran down the long corridor, which led to the imposing mahogany staircase. Portraits of people who Victoria had never known frowned upon her through ornate frames. She vowed never to sit for such a depiction. What could cause such ominous scowls? She thought for a moment about slithering down the black bannister. It was something she did often as a young girl, but her 5'5" delicate frame was not suited for such folly.

"Good morning father." Victoria gently bussed her father before taking her seat at the dining table. She sunk into the ivory upholstered chair, which had become accustomed to her form. Her place was designated between her two sisters who were first to arrive. Peter sat alone across the table and father took the head. Mother's chair remained vacant due to her travels.

"Good Morning Victoria. You are late to arrive which has become the custom. Peter is about to lead prayer. You are just in time."

Victoria smiled at young Elaine who was rarely at a loss for words. Elaine was at times a plaything to her older siblings but even Elaine herself knew it was heartfelt affection. She enjoyed the ribbing, as it gave her relevance among the Tompkins children.

"God bless all present and Dear Mother, may she be safe in her travels. Please make the food sustaining and palatable. Amen."

"Clever Peter. You always have a way of getting to the significant part. Your brevity is appreciated, although the words are hardly prosaic."

"Thank you Victoria." Peter waited until Father and his sisters were served before he devoured his oysters and bacon.

"I am happy to see you all this morning. We have no callers today. With your Mother at Persimmon House, I thought it best we not receive today. I am certain you can all busy yourselves on a sunny day. I gave notice at the stables should any of you wish to ride the grounds. I may take a jaunt myself. I would like to have tea with you Victoria, in my study at half past three"

"Yes father. I plan to stroll the hop gardens but I will plan tea. I promise to be timely. I will alert Esther of my engagements."

*****

Victoria spent the day on the many acres gardens of the Markham Estate. It was her favorite spot, encircled with stonewalls covered in early spring hops. Azalea beds showed no bloom as of yet but they would burst in bright hues come summer. As Victoria walked, she dreamed of life beyond the Estate grounds. She welcomed what London would bring. The adventures ahead seemed endless. Victoria was unaware that the machinations of the Earl and Countess. As her parents they had already forged a path towards her future.

At 17 and the eldest of 3 girls it was dictated by society that a suitable mate be found for carefree Victoria. Peter was the male heir. He would inherit the title of Earl and everything that would entail including land

and other assets. A man of means and title would care for Victoria. She would provide him with an ample flock of descendants. Dreams of ambling down the Champs Ellysees with a man whom she loved were to be just that – dreams. It was not an urgent reality. She remained blissful.

"Come along now Victoria. Your Father will look for you at half past. We must begin our journey back to the house. You have a time for a quick refresher before tea."

"Always prompt Esther. We must arrange for a change of fragrance. I am tired of Lavender. It has become too youthful and common. I prefer something mature. Fetch me some samples as the week passes. More sophisticated and dare I say – alluring."

Esther laughed, amused by the request.

****

"Hello Father. I am weary from the afternoon and ravenous." Victoria fell onto the cushioned sofa.

"My dear Victoria, I need not ask you to make yourself comfortable."

"If you expect formality you u have chosen the wrong Tompkins to join you to tea." Victoria filled her mouth with smoked salmon on toast. It was rare to have tea alone with her Father in his study. It was a dark and comfortable room. To be invited to his inner sanctum was an honor. Books lined the shelves, which reached the ceiling. She imagined he had read them all, as he was not one for show in his private space.

"Victoria, we anticipate your mother's arrival home by next week end. Any longer and I worry she will never find her way back to Dover. She gets lost in the excitement of London as the season approaches."

"I shall welcome her of course. She will need time to recover before we should receive visitors. The staff will be alerted. Everything will be in place for her return to Markham. Is there anything specific I should arrange upon her return?" Victoria shifted as she expected to receive instructions.

"We will receive a caller the day following the Countesses return. He is a gentleman. He is Lord Hawthorne from the upper region of Kent. He has joined us for a hunt in years past here at the estate. He travels with his brother, Lord Damian. He is a widow and a pal from years ago. Victoria, he is a dear friend similar in years to me and a man of superior manners."

"Yes father. I shall make plans for his arrival. Are overnight accommodations required?"

"Juliet and Samuel are preparing quarters for them. I will expect you to be dressed in your finest attire for receiving a guest of his high honor. Preparations have already begun for Lord Hawthorne's arrival."

Victoria became confused by the grandeur behind Lord Hawthorne's visit. She awaited her Father's explanation.

"My dear daughter, you are to be married to Lord Hawthorne."

"Oh." Ann was speechless and astonished by her father's announcement. She was not planning to be promised to another before laying eyes upon him. Her dreams only hours past were unattainable musings. A man her father's age was a sour joke. "No father." Her face grew wet in reaction to the horrible news.

"Your Mother and I have considered the matter carefully. It is to be Victoria. Lord Hawthorne can provide you with substantial wealth and a proper place in society. You are betrothed to Lord James Hawthorne. Go to your quarters and rest up before dinner. Allow time for the shock of the announcement to settle in."

"I ask to be excused from dinner father. The day has proved too much."

"Good day Victoria. I will see you when the sun rises on a new day. You know what is expected."

****

Victoria returned to her room and collapsed on a chaise. She was devastated with a hyperventilating fit. Drops fell from her eyes. Esther came to console the sweet girl she helped bring into the world. She cradled Victoria's head in her fleshy arms.

"Esther, I must tell you what my parents have done. They…." Victoria was cut off.

"I knew this was coming me dear. I was powerless."

"Oh, Esther. You knew and you held it a secret? You are like me mum. How could you keep secrets? The whole world is against me."

"I let you dream. I could not devastate you with the impeding arrangement."

"I will not be happy. I will wish for the day I die."

CHAPTER TWO

Lady Victoria woke up on Sunday morning. It was six am and the room was still shrouded in darkness. The sound of the rain soothed Victoria. She almost believed she was deep in a dream, as though the day prior never happened. She closed her eyes to rewind the past. She sprang to reality as her younger sister Mary entered her chambers.

"Hello Victoria. May I come in to snuggle. I am scared of the torrid rain and fierce winds. Mother is not about. The sounds caused such a fright." Mary stood before the bed still in her sleep gown and cap.

"Of course little Mary. You may be just what I needed. You know that you are always welcome to come along."

Elaine was not far behind. The Tompkins steps, as they were referred due to their closeness in age, were tight knit. The Tompkins gathered like this when one was frightened or sad. The others just knew the need intuitively. The nasty weather made a good excuse to come together. Victoria's bed was not short on comforts so it was often the place to join.

"Well, I see I am the last to arrive. Have a spot?"

"We would not forget you Peter. We promise not to tell your chums you were scared of the thunder." Elaine loved to chide her brother.

Each of the children had their own maid. Most of them had been on board since their birth. By now, they knew where the children were. It was their routine to let them be. Victoria had the largest quarters and the most luxurious bed. She had a penchant for fine linens and her area included a large sleeping room, two parlors, a changing area and washroom containing a large tub and two washstands. It was never explained why there were two of the former. The gardens could be viewed out the wall of windows and when the fog lifted, the White Cliffs of Dover could be seen. The Dover Cliffs gave way to the strait separating England from France.

"The imposing winds are those of change. Are they not Victoria?" Peter readjusted himself to save from falling to the floor.

"You must have heard of the arrangement, Peter."

"Yes, father gave us the details at last night's meal. He had to explain your absence. Tell me you knew of plans for you and Lord Hawthorne to wed?" Mary said tentatively. She knew she was next.

"No Mary. I was made aware yesterday at afternoon tea. I am betrothed to Lord Hawthorne. A man I have barely come acquaintance with. A man of more than 60 years. Father's age." Victoria began to sob but contained herself. "I am 17 years of age. It is to be expected that I marry but I only wished for a small parcel of love to be included in the matter. Peter you are to be married to the demure Jane Marley. Love has grown there, it is felt."

I am fortunate to hold a future with Jane. Mother and father have hopes of the same for you and Lord Hawthorne. He will provide for your richest fancies. You will provide him with a male heir who will be your guard in later years. Your trunks will be full with finery collected as you travel the continent abroad."

"We shall invite him in five days' time. Mother will return also. The event will be worthy."

"Yes Victoria we shall have much fun preparing for Lord Hawthorne's arrival." Elaine chimed in.

Victoria sighed.

****

"Victoria my dear, your father has delayed breakfast enough. The others are back in their rooms making preparations. We have to get you dressed. Your father has met with the staff. We shall have the full complement available to ready the estate for Lord Hawthorne and your Mother. It is like holiday and we have less than a week's time to prepare."

Lady Victoria and Esther fought quickly and got her prepared for the day. Victoria was bustle free. She and her siblings would be spending the days with the secretary and governess. They would deliver a flood of etiquette protocol.

Peter was dressed fashionably in a calf length jacket in deep burgundy. His short-cropped hair and well-manicured burns made him appear beyond his 18 years. He proceeded down the grey hallway for deportment instruction. He thought the entire process needless, as he had grown up in a formal household. He had become aware of the proper way to proceed.

"Hello Lydia. I suppose you are to instruct Peter and I on how to proceed in the coming months. You and Clara need not waste your precious time. I am sure it will be months until I am to wed. Peter has been entwined in the matter for some time with Jane Marley."

Lydia and Clara had been among the Tompkins family for considerable time. They shared a glance. They knew what Lady Victoria had not yet come to know. Her marriage to Lord Hawthorne was to take place two days after the man's arrival at Markham. They would be sharing a first turn in the ballroom in less than one week. They would conceal the secret at the Earl's request.

It was perhaps a dangerous game to begin plans for a marriage without alerting the betrothed. The Earl and Countess had discussed the matter with Lord Hawthorne. He would not be open to a year's long engagement due to his advancing age. A male heir was necessary and it was hoped Lady Victoria would be able to provide.

"Lady Victoria. You realize that you will be leaving your days of folly behind you. Your life with Lord Hawthorne at the Manor will come with its share of responsibility and decorum. Much of it you are already attuned to but we will refresh you in the coming days. You will meet the honorable Lord Hawthorne and receive a ring this weekend. Then you shall officially be engaged and you are welcome to enjoy a courtship until the wedding, after which you will be open for privacies with your husband."

"Yes Lydia, I am aware that until such wedding I am not to be alone with my betrothed. I will follow regulations such that Peter has shared with Jane. He has had a one-year engagement that will result in his summer's wedding. I can expect the same measure of time. I have not been advised otherwise."

"Lady" Lydia gently avoided the subject.

"Peter. Do any questions remain for you in this matter? You have had many opportunities to get to know Miss Marley through visitations and carriage outings. After the official event in summer you will make your home in the house at Granger within the Estate. Arrangements are being made so that it be a safe transition for you and the new Lady Tompkins. You will defer to her on much entailing receiving callers and responding to requests. She will surely be with child in the near future. That will change things and you will receive maids to assist."

"Yes dear Lydia." Peter spoke with exaggeration and a flamboyant bow.

The remainder of the session was devoted to behavior expected at the formal dinner welcoming Lord Hawthorne. He would be accompanied by his brother and constant companion, Lord Henley. His private butler and daughters would accompany him also and several of the Earl's staff would be assigned to his wishes. The dinner would be proceeded by introductions and exchange of rings between him and Lady Victoria. The wedding date would be approximated at that time.

Mary and Elaine would be witness to all. They should follow in coming years and would learn from the events.

****

The events of the week had been a flurry of preparations. Tomorrow would be Saturday, marked by the arrival of Lord Hawthorne and his company by noon. Mother would be pleased by the arrangements. Her presence had been missed but the staff grew in size by triplicate and all worked tediously to arrive at perfection.

The Tompkins girls were given the day to wander and enjoy being a troop of carefree sprites for one final time. They had decided to join in the stables and to take mount to the cliffs. The horses would be dressed and readied for the ride. Benjamin, a trusted and humorous member of the staff would accompany them. He was a good-natured. The girls shared stories amongst themselves on such rides and Benjamin respected their intimacy.

"Benjamin. Hello friend. You poor thing must listen to our gossip once more."

"My Lady Victoria. There is little left to surprise me amongst you three. I know more than allowed but your chatter is not repeated."

"Promise you will never change your ways Benjamin."

"I want Cadyleggs for my own." Mary blew into the stables. She waved her crop within inches of whipping Benjamin on the face. She was sensible in a grey dress with peplum. Green velvet piping surrounded the brim of her hat. She appeared born to the saddle.

"Cadyleggs is ready for you Lady. I see you have your crop available." Benjamin smiled.

Elaine joined the group. "I will ride whichever you have chosen for me. I so dislike the mare I rode last month. She was of horrible temperament and caused such within me."

"The mare you mention has been set to pasture due to said temperament. We shall have you upon Sadie,"

"Benjamin, you mean the poor mare has been put under the ground we walk upon." Victoria declared.

"You know too much Lady Victoria."

"Is True."

"Are we all set to ride ladies? I have lunch provisions but we need to begin our journey to the White Cliffs to make it back before sundown."

The three Tompkins sisters and Benjamin started towards their destination. The day was full of mist and mystery. It always was, when they visited the cliffs. The white chalk-like facades gave way to the green sea and beyond that the passage to France. Victoria' imagination ran wild like the grasses and thistles of the landscape. It represented longing and waiting as it served as the spot for warship returns. It could be a sad place but it touched Victoria in a different way. It seemed a place of waiting which could lead to a life renewed.

Benjamin led the ladies on their journey.

"Do you remember your previous meeting with Lord Hawthorne?" Mary began the talk of Victoria's situation, as it was heavy on everyone's mind.

"I do not, as Father has had so many callers throughout the years. No rumors have come before me."

"He may be a fat man. He is sure not to hold his own teeth. Oh Victoria, what to imagine." Elaine scared herself with the possibilities.

"Enough! I have only one day before I am formally introduced. I imagine Mother and Father would not betroth me to a hideous man. He had a wife once who produced him two daughters so I do not believe him to be that terrible."

The ladies pick nicked in a clearing with an endless view of the sea before them. It was mild and the skies were in general free of clouds. Benjamin served them some meat sandwiches and cheese. They shared a fine bar of chocolate and reminisced. It was an agreeable outing before the formality of life interrupted. Benjamin took a few sips from his canteen to steady himself and joined in the conversation when invited.

They arrived back at the Estate by sunset. A quick dinner was had by all and each retreated for a rest before the arrivals.

***

Lady Victoria was awake by nine. She dressed in a green dress, which included lace accents on the high collar. A lighter green velvet encircled the bottom of her skirt, which just skimmed the floor. Her frock showed a flat front with subtle ruching below the waist. Before the dress, she was tightly secured in a corset. Her silhouette was slender as a result. She had held tightly to the bedpost while Esther securely laced her up. She was bustled in back. She felt like a sausage in an ill-fitting casing.

She applied a bit of powder. Makeup was not necessary for such a young face. Women of her place in society wore very little as a standard. Most days were spent in doors and sleep was bountiful so little was needed. Victoria adorned her neck with a cameo necklace. Jeweled emerald earrings hung from her lobes. She wore no ring. That place would soon be occupied. Esther arranged her golden hair straight back with gentle ringlets gathered at the nape. Finally, she laced up her boots, adapted with small heels.

"Esther, I think I am complete. If I am not, there is little more I can accomplish. This will have to serve." Lady Victoria stood before the mirror with more a frown than smile.

"You must be hopeful my Lady. The trauma will pass. You must at least try to enjoy the present, as it serves as a corridor to the future. Without that, you have nothing. Oh no dear, do not cry now. There, there – my delicate peach,"

Lady Victoria, sobbed in her trusted maid's arms.

***

The Countess had arrived back at Markham Estate at 11 am and she had time to refresh and change into proper attire for welcoming Lord Hawthorne. Lady Victoria, Lord Peter, Mary and Elaine settled into the parlor. The footmen and the butler were on hand. The Countess had her personal maid present and the housekeeper was in attendance.

Throughout the home staff was hidden around every corner. They were alerted should the need arise which was not likely considering the detailed planning completed.

Victoria was relieved when Father took his position in the heavily appointed parlor. Kind words were exchanged while they awaited Lord Hawthorne and his entourage.

"I present to you Lord Thomas Hawthorne and………………"

Victoria did not hear the remaining introductions. She focused on her husband to be. She swallowed hard and took in what stood before her.

Lord Thomas Hawthorne was a man of ample width. Some may describe him rotund. He had a doughy face that was clean-shaven except for wild burns. They lanced down to his dimples, which Victoria only guessed he had. He wore a "stovepipe" hat that showed hair beneath that was surely grey. He walked with a cane that was necessary. His eyes were lost under his brow and Victoria guessed they were brown. He was dressed in appropriate attire of a three-piece suit with wide burgundy tie. Lord

Hawthorne was short of breath after the short walk from his carriage.

He bowed before Lady Victoria. She extended her hand and he gave it a dry kiss. There was a formal ivory colored chair directly opposite Victoria's where Lord Hawthorne took presence.

The Earl made a formal introduction of intentions. They were details worked out ahead of time. Victoria had no say in the matter so she did not listen closely.

Two footmen stepped forward and assisted Lord Hawthorne. He kneeled upon a brocade pillow and placed a ring of engagement on Lady Victoria's finger.

With a nod, papers were brought forth for signatures of the Earl, Countess and Lord Hawthorne.

"We shall move on to the dining room for a magnificent feast next. First, the gentlemen will join me in the drawing room. You ladies may take time to acquaint yourselves here in the parlor before we commence."

Lord Hawthorne's daughters, Hannah and Sophie, were of about Victoria's age. They were polite, while likely bewildered by the pace of the events.

"We welcome you to the family and to our home at Derby Manor. My sister and I will be siblings to you if you take account of our ages. We will have such fun filling the manor with many new additions to the family." Sophie was welcoming. It must feel odd to accept a new Lady of the Manor with such similar age.

"Yes, your assistance will be needed to make the transition smooth. We will have sufficient time; I am sure, before the wedding."

Glances were exchanged rapidly, by all in attendance. Lady Victoria noticed nothing.

***

The dining room was set perfectly for twelve. Father at the head of the table, as host. The finest china and fine silver were formally placed. Beautiful floral arrangements of lilies and hyacinth were placed on either end of the sideboard in the finest crystal vases. Loaves of hearty bread baked at the estate waited to be devoured. The condiments were placed in fine vessels.

Each setting included at least six glasses to accommodate the numerous toasts planned. Forks held varying number of tines. There were knives for cutting, buttering and slicing.

All were placed on the magnificent walnut table that was polished to show reflection. Each setting was placed on delicate doilies.

"Welcome to Lord Hawthorne." The Earl continued to mention all in his entourage. "We are pleased to bring these families together through the wedding of honorable Lord Thomas Hawthorne and Lady Victoria Tompkins" Victoria hung on her father's final words "to take place two days hence here at Markham Estate."

All eyes were upon Lady Victoria. She remained seated in utter astonishment.

CHAPTER THREE

Victoria was lingering in bed while she digested the events as they had unfolded the evening before. Her face was sore, as she had held a grin for many hours. It was as good as that of a stage actress. Falsified to please the Earl, Countess, Lord Hawthorne and all else in attendance. She dearly loved her parents and pleasing them and the rest of society was of the utmost importance.

Lord Hawthorne was a shock. His resemblance to a troll could not be more exact. He was pleasant, almost jolly, which was enhanced by the numerous toasts presented at dinner. He laughed with such intensity that Lady Victoria swore she heard his false teeth rattle. Mary was obsessed with the matter of dentures. She rumored that they were teeth stolen from a young corpse to display a new set in the mouths of the wealthy. Victoria shuddered at the thought of kissing such a mouth. Surely, there would be some manner in which to avoid this.

Victoria was chaste and images of sharing embrace with Lord Hawthorne were unimaginable. She read of romance in poetry. She was excited at the imagine of love. The future differed from her private visions of a rapturous passion. It was a mystery that she should remain unsolved. Heirs were anticipated and unpleasant chores would be completed.

Victoria cried softly in her dark room. It was the only place she could release in such a manner. The loss she felt was too much to tolerate. She buried her face in a cushion.

***

"Good morning Esther," Victoria smiled as her ally quietly entered. "I should think we have a full schedule of events today. Please advise me, so I should know the timing of the preparations. I am but a child and in two days, I shall be a wife. Please hold my hand through it all as I am short of experience."

"Lady Victoria, I am aware. I have been aware and I promised not to advise you of the quick schedule. As a result, planning has previously gotten under way."

"Esther why did you keep the truth from *me*? I am aware of the predicament that you were in but I would have thought our closeness would have meant more. I feel lost and with little time to find my way. I am here for your instruction Esther."

"My Lady. I cherish you and I will trust your confidence on matters hence. I was supposed to remain here at Markham and bid farewell to you. You were to retain a new staff at Derby with Lord Hawthorne. A new personal entourage including maid."

"Oh no Esther. That would interfere with any hopes I have remaining. You are a mum to me. I have much to bear and without you, I shall be incapable. That would be true torture. I do not think I could manage the stress of producing an heir. Please tell me you informed Mother and Father of the impossibility of such plans."

"It was a delicate negotiation but I managed. Your parents are aware of the stress that you will endure. My Lady, you have not have had to manage much through your youth and the changes will be severe."

"Yes Esther, I am aware." Victoria was by now dressed in sensible grey. It was easy to remove. She would be getting her costume fitted in preparation for the wedding. She would spend hours standing in her undergarments until they suited the dress to fit her form. It would be the one worn by her own mother 20 years prior.

The house would be prepared for the wedding day. Peter was planning to hold a massive ball in the early summer for his wedding to Jane but this affair would be more understated. The couple would hold a ceremony at the church in Dover. Lady Victoria would arrive by carriage at noon. The groom and his attendants would be waiting, having arrived by their own carriage. After the ceremony, the husband and wife would receive well- wishers followed by a ceremony in the ballroom.

***

"Hello my dear Victoria." The Countess Maria was waiting in the parlor for her daughter.

"Mother" Victoria gave her mother a gentle kiss. She fancied a cup of tea. She was accommodated by Juliet, who wore many hats among the household staff. She was favored by the Countess, as she was expert at anticipating her needs. "Thank you Juliet."

"That will be all for now. Please leave Lady Victoria and I alone to discuss amongst ourselves."

Juliet exited the room and left mother and daughter to discuss what was expected in the coming days. The Countess was not typical in the way she mothered. She handled family like an extension of society. There were only four Tompkins children, which was scant in number and fell short of expectation. She was aware of this and devoted herself to a larger picture to retain her relevance. Her children all loved and held her in high esteem but the Countess served as a figurehead.

"My dear Victoria, I realize you became betrothed to the honorable Lord Hawthorne rather abruptly. I am glad you seem well rested and willing to accept your new husband. The matter weighed on your father and I. We arrived at the decision after long consideration. You will be among the upper tier of English society as Lady Hawthorne. Your needs will be met and the respect you receive will be tremendous."

Victoria cringed. She had few concerns about society if it required closeness to a man she did not love or know beyond a brief introduction.

"Yes Mother."

"As you have no choice in the matter we shall continue with preparations."

"Yes Mother."

"Victoria my dear daughter there is one point that must be clearly made. Lord Hawthorne is a father to two ladies, which is all his wife was able to produce before a premature death. He spent years heartbroken before he realized the urgent need for a male heir. You have many years of child bearing to provide Derby Manor with children. It is your duty to serve."

"I understand the urgency mum."

With the matter settled, they would discuss the plans. Victoria was not asked to toil, as the staff would handle arrangements. Her dress was ivory with dainty appliques and lace coming up to a high neckline. An intricate bustle covered the back. It was an addition on her mother's dress to accommodate the current fashion. Her figure would be tightly bound with a corset resulting in a tiny waist. Her mother purchased the dress, custom designed from Paris. For weeks before she departed for Persimmon House she and Juliet had worked with the tailor to amend the frock. The hoops that mother had worn with the dress had been removed. Numerous layers of cotton and gauze petticoats were added. The sleeves were long and ballooned out at top and fitted past the wrist with cotton detail.

Since it had been worn twenty years prior, it would be considered "something old" to follow tradition. She would follow with an azure and white handkerchief showing her maiden name initials. Lady Sterling was loaning her the veil. She would hold a coin in her shoe for luck and prosperity. Victoria had imagined following such tradition would be fun. It was duty.

Victoria was not certain how Lord Hawthorne would appear but it was sure to be appropriate. He would surely be wearing a suit of three pieces with an ascot. At that moment, it occurred to Victoria that she never referred to him as Thomas. Peter referred to his lady as Jane and even occasionally, he would utter "My Sweet Jane" or "Janey". She had heard the

Countess mention her father as John. She found it odd that she should ever call him by his given name.

"Mother I should like to view the ballroom, where the reception should be held. I just require a peek."

"You may go without me. I will rest until we begin our fitting. Juliet will meet us in my changing room."

Lady Victoria was off to see the formal setting as it was prepared. She loved the ballroom when it was well appointed for an occasion. It was always a happy time when such an event occurred. This would be different.

CHAPTER FOUR

The day of the wedding arrived. Victoria was served a bite, carried in by Esther. It included simple fare of sweet rolls and some cheese from the dairy. It was to suffice until after 3 pm, when she would sit at the reception as Lady Thomas Hawthorne. The moniker was still difficult to imagine let alone utter. She drank the tea, which accompanied her meal. It was made of hibiscus flower or some other brew the staff had procured from the city. There was a cozy importer located in the center of London specializing in all types to suit a variety of palates and dispositions.

"Esther please tell me the sun should shine. It is my wedding day and I deserve a little glow in the sky."

"It is a grey day but it may change as time passes. We shall remain hopeful. Your dress turned out lovely. It took the night before Juliet and the seamstress made it perfect. The young ladies will wear their white lace tiered dresses they had prepared at the end of last summer. The satin ribbons in their hair will complement their necklaces and sapphire earrings. Mary will be very snuggly bound as she is quickly growing into a woman. Her figure has outgrown the form of the costume but we made sufficient alterations. We shall arrange your jewelry while you glance at the expected attendants. There will not be but 100 guests in attendance. Time did not allow for a grand affair. Not to worry my Lady. Shall be a memorable celebration." Esther spoke from Victoria's vanity bench. She rarely sat down. Her exhaustion from the flurry of activity showed.

"Oh Esther, the wedding is not of concern. The smile shall tell my lie. You and I shall be the only ones aware of my misery. My concern will come later. Consummation of the whole affair will be expected. The man will see me like no one but myself and perhaps you have seen. The scene will not be one I have dreamed. It was all a young girl's fantasy." Victoria sobbed again. It had become routine.

Victoria had a stream of visitors that morning. Mary and Elaine popped in for a chat. Both seemed overcome with worry. There was a pallor faking happiness throughout the estate home.

"Dear sister, you are so calm in spirit. I do not know how I shall ever mimic the same should I become betrothed to an old man like Lord Hawthorne. He is a bit of an old sot I believe. It is prior to ten and he has been taking a drink." Mary loved to spread news. She waited for Victoria's response.

"Mary, you have at least a years' time before arrangements for you are undertaken. Mother and Father are so concerned with Peter and myself. They should need a rest I think. As for Lord Hawthorne, I worry not. He is a convivial old chap. I should think nothing poor of the man if he should partake in a bracer." Victoria stood waiting for a comment from her younger sister. She tended to mimic her sister when at a loss for words.

"Victoria, you are going to be missed here at Markham," Elaine began to whimper. Victoria was careful not to join in, although the thought had temped her.

"Well, look it is my lovely daughters. We are having a chance spell to meet together."

"Yes Mother. Come join us." Esther was by now preparing tea for the whole company of the Tompkins ladies.

"Are you girls all prepared to step into your dresses? It shall be a well-timed event. Lady Sterling and her entourage arrived at my same time. They are by now settled in one of the guest cottages down the road. Victoria, you shall see all of your cousins. Some you have not laid eyes on since summer last. We did have a grand time at lawn games and folly. Lady Diane is swollen with child and near to giving birth. Lady Sarah is betrothed to the Duke of Canterbury. The Honorable Barry Lange and his brothers will be present. They are all very appropriate men not yet married."

Elaine and Mary shared a glance. It seemed that the gentleman mentioned may be appropriate mates for the girls. It sounded interesting to them, as they were under 60 years of age. At this stage in their development, the mention of any male name caught their attention. Victoria was similar in the past but now all her dreams were nonsense. She was resigned.

The Countess continued. "The Baron will be present. He is recently widowed and will be accompanied by the honorable Madeline and his other daughter Suzanne. Many of the Tully's will be present from Dover and the

Viscount Herbert Manly and the Viscountess are to arrive by carriage from Essex. We were short on time so many of our acquaintances from Paris and beyond did not make the journey. You shall see them at London. You shall be Lady Hawthorne by then and all will be looking at you for evidence of child. It is so exciting my sweet Victoria."

"Yes mother. It sounds divine. I am sure to forget all of the names present. I will rely on your counsel." Victoria spoke gently.

"I shall be at your side throughout. I have given you the names of many of the finest invited. I believe the Duke of Wellington will be present. Him you may not have seen. He is at every society event. He is known for his conquests. He is nothing at all, really, just a title."

"The name means nothing. You shall point the creature out to me." Victoria brushed off most of the names. It was not the first thing on her mind.

****

Lord Hawthorne was in his quarters that the staff had finely appointed for his stay at the

Markham Estate. He was sitting at the massive mahogany desk at the center of the adjacent parlor. Fountain pen in hand, he was finalizing some correspondence and business before he and his Lady should retreat for a short sojourn. They would arrive at the seaside by weeks end and spend two restful fortnights, returning to Derby before social season in London. There were certain personal matters he enjoyed penning. He would leave most of the work up to his secretary Martha. She was a mannerly spinster whom he trusted implicitly. She and his butler, James were his constant companions since the death of his wife.

"Lord Hawthorne should you need anything while you write. I dare not intrude on your privacy again until it is time to journey to the church in Dover. Your suit of clothes is prepared ahead for you. I can see you are otherwise ready to be wed. We should travel to a home for the night on the backside of the estate. Quarters are prepared for you and the next Lady Thomas Hawthorne. You should be in private except for Samuel of the estate staff, Martha and myself who will be at hand should the need arise."

"There will be nothing more my trusted friend. I am sure it goes without mention, but be sure to have fires well stoked in all rooms. There will be drink at hand?"

"Yes my Lord." With a smile and easy bow, John quietly disappeared.

Lord Hawthorne was in a solemn mood. He was marrying Lady Victoria as a matter of business. He desired to produce an heir and the match was suitable. He reminisced about the prior Lady June whom he had married when he was just a boy. It was a hopeful time and there was a hint of love surrounding their engagement. She was sweet and demure not unlike the Lady Victoria. They had a future of producing many children to fill their home at Derby Manor. Sophie and Hannah had come easily but his dear wife got fever while the two girls were still in nappies. She suffered in a fragile state until she expired in Lord Hawthorne's embrace. A tear stained his freshly penned note.

"John, drink please!" He roared and caught John's ear who was quick to respond with a heavy glass of fine gin.

****

Victoria was dressed in her wedding gown nearly ready for her carriage. Her mother would ride with her to the church in Dover. Father Cecil would perform the ceremony as he had for the Earl and Countess years earlier. Math would prove his age to be quite advanced. He had been calling on many occasions and performed baptism on all of the Tompkins children. He was like an uncle to the family. He would follow all protocol properly and hardly needed to read a script.

"Mother, did you bring along the veil? I am otherwise fully prepared. I am tight in my corset and with so many petticoats I am sure to be covered sufficiently." Victoria spoke quickly.

"I have the veil from your Auntie Rose. It will reach the floor." The Countess displayed the breathtaking gossamer garment. It was embroidered in intricate lace and appeared less than its years. The Countess had worn it 20 years prior and Victoria would be standing before her daughter with the veil in hand in 20 hence. Her mother had it attached to a coronet encircled in delicate peach roses. The type found growing wild on the white cliffs. She placed the ornament on Victoria's crown. Perfect.

It may not be the finest day for Victoria's heart but she looked lovely. She wore simple diamonds dangling from her ears and a necklace with an ivory cameo surrounded by diamonds. She would have on the ring given to her by Lord Hawthorne only two days prior. She still had to have it amended by the jeweler to fit her dainty fingers. It was a single emerald stone, which was large. It was cut with angles so it shined in the light. It was not to go unnoticed. Victoria admired the bauble. Anyone who knew her would have chosen a sapphire, simple and sparkling like her eyes.

"You impress me Victoria. You make a radiant bride. The carriage will be waiting. It has been decorated for the day by the staff at the stables. Benjamin chose particular horses. He made sure the manes were perfect, as it was for his Lady Victoria."

"I am sure Benjamin showed his devotion. He is a fine member of the staff here at the estate."

Victoria walked down the grey hallway. She passed the portraits, finally knowing why they frowned upon her. Like her, freedom had been denied them. Decisions had been made, followed by arrangements and then - Victoria need not imagine, as it was all a finely laid plan.

Lady Victoria walked down the opulent staircase through the marble foyer to her waiting transport. Her mother was inside upon her arrival. It would be a short journey to the church. Victoria was ready.

****

The church was grey stone. Vines climbed the ancient walls, allowed to grow with abandon. It was topped by an enormous bell tower that rang to announce the occasion. The audience was not large, as most would head directly to the estate for the reception. Her Aunt Lady Sterling was there with her children. She got a peak of the others but her focus was needed towards Lord Hawthorne. He stood at the end of the aisle, which was made of cold brownish bricks. Her parents had performed the same duty twenty years ago. It was Victoria's turn.

Formal vows were exchanged as Father Cecil presided.

"Now Lord Thomas Hawthorne, I give to you Lady Victoria to be your wife from now through eternity. May you be blessed with many kin."

Thomas leaned in to give Victoria a kiss. It was no finer than Lady Hawthorne had anticipated and she would never put a drink of gin to her mouth again.

****

The table in the ballroom was beautifully set with fine white china and fine crystal. Champagne from France was ready to pour. Roses were nestled in vases and wall sconces throughout. They were early blooms taken from the grounds. The light pink variety were always Victoria's favorites. They were so innocent. Perhaps, she thought, red roses may be more appropriate in the future.

She and Lord Hawthorne would be seated at the center of the table with her parents and their other family members. The guest would perambulate through the room. Velvet couches were casually placed near the tapestry covered walls. Victoria and Thomas would make it through the crowd to greet well-wishers. A legion of toasts would be made to the newly married pair.

There was a string quartet playing. It was meant to be listened to, but it was mainly present for ambiance. The Earl favored the violin. He had made sure each of the Tompkins children were given lessons from the time they could clutch the instrument. None of the four had a predilection for the violin.

"You look well Lady Hawthorne, I can see by your rosy glow that marriage has already agreed upon you."

"Oh yes Viscount I should be very happy to begin life at Derby Manor with Lord Hawthorne and the Ladies Hannah and Sophie. The whole affair is enchanting."

Victoria smiled, "enchanting"? She must stop thinking of this as a fairy tale. She was married to a troll, albeit an amiable one. Lord Hawthorne was by her side but engaged in a different conversation with the Viscountess. Victoria was flanked on the other side by the Countess. Her mother was born to social events such as this. Her eyes were in constant motion. She was taking mental note of all present. She could procure a great deal of gossip from such an event.

Victoria and Thomas made their way towards the cake table. There was a large mountain of a cake with tiers that would go uneaten. Lord and Lady Hawthorne each had a separate smaller cake. Victoria's was frosted in buttercream topped with delicate pansies. Lord Hawthorne had requested a dark chocolate cake. It was round and fat. It resembled him.

Earl of Markham Estate raised a glass to toast Lord and Lady Hawthorne. Victoria was bored. She glanced across the room.

****

He was a tall man of six feet. His face was clean-shaven and his flaxen hair well groomed but showed a charming cowlick. His broad shoulders gave way to a wasp waist. He was elegantly turned out, with a morning coat and pinstriped dark grey trousers. A cardinal red ascot was pinned with a single pearl. He had his own teeth and they were white. Victoria did not recognize the face. He was without an escort. The man who she had never before seen smiled at Victoria. His eyes were fixed upon her. They were fresh and green. Victoria nodded.

He was the Duke of Wellington.

****

The evening finished according to plan. Victoria returned to her quarters to change into sensible dress for the short ride to the far back of the estate. It was to be the place where she and her new husband would physically confirm their vows.

Victoria removed her embroidered stockings and replaced them with a fresh, more sensible pair. She put on a modest olive dress. The bustle was decorated with black velvet piping. She put on a pair of black button boots. She had worn flat slippers with her wedding dress that fit her feet well. Her boots were always a size six when her feet were a gigantic size seven. It was a custom of fashion she did not favor.

Out of habit, she fell into a daydream. She could not rid her mind of the man she had glimpsed at the reception. She grew hot. It was not in anticipation of her husband.

"I am ready to depart Esther. I must meet my husband, as we are to depart for our wedding night."

"I have prepared your things. Everything you require is laid out for you. I am to remain here. Staff has been arranged for you."

"Oh Esther, please accompany me."

"I may not my Lady. I am to stay behind to prepare your trunks for the honeymoon at Budleigh. I have been by your side. I believe you are primed for the occasion."

"I suppose I have no say in the matter. I am Lord Hawthorne's now"

Victoria and Thomas took their seats opposite one another in the carriage. It was the first time they had been alone together. He removed his black satin top hat, which was another first. His hair resembled filthy wet sand. It was dampened by the sweat appearing at his temples and making its way down his sideburns. He smelled of gin and cigars.

"Hello Victoria. You are *my* wife." Lord Hawthorne appeared pleased with himself.

"I am. I am yours Lord Hawthorne. I shall call you Thomas in private. I believe that is protocol between husband and wife."

"That will do until you come upon a pet name. June called me "Prince". You may use it if you like. June was a lovely wife."

"I am sure the first Lady Hawthorne was worthy, Thomas."

They entered the brick cottage. The fire was lit in the parlor and a decanter was filled with red wine. Two silver stemmed chalices were placed before a platter of chocolates.

"James! Gin. I do not enjoy wine before sleep. It does not sit well with my digestion." Thomas growled as he stuffed a chocolate in his mouth.

Lord Hawthorne sat on a crimson and gold chaise before the fireplace. He invited Victoria to join him. She acquiesced and made herself comfortable. She passed on the sweets and wine. Lord Hawthorne pulled at the scooped neck of her dress, pulling at the tight laces. He was admiring her bust and a small drop of drool fell from the corner of his fleshy lips. He sucked in his slobber and caught her gaze.

"You have saved all for me?"

"Yes my Lord."

Lord Hawthorne removed his formal coat and tie. He unstrapped his braces. Victoria did not move, for she knew not how to.

With that, Thomas took a healthy drink of gin. Lord Hawthorne found the comfort of the chaise again. He slept.

Victoria notified James of her Lord's state. He knowingly sprang to action and got the man to bed.

"You have sleeping chambers down the same corridor. A door joins them but you should not worry about privacy. We will see you at morning meal. Bea will be in at 10 to assist you. If you should need anything, alert Bea by the chime next to your bed. Good night Lady Hawthorne." James lowered his head and departed.

The marriage would remain unconsummated.

CHAPTER FIVE

Victoria woke up Lady Hawthorne. All had not been a nightmare. It was odd not to have Esther visit her. She always shared her nighttime dreams with her maid. Esther was so much more than a servant. She trusted her above all else. For today, it would be Bea. Victoria would appear jovial and well rested. Of course, she would not mention the encounter with Lord Hawthorne that did not happen. She would become practiced at the lie.

Victoria looked out at the misty morning. The wedding night was spent in a small home on Markham. The area was near the boundary line of the property. Peat fields and non-descript yarrow patches covered rolling hills. The sky was purple and the scene took on a mysterious nature. Victoria rather liked it. It suited her mood. She thought of the stranger at the wedding ceremony. It was dangerous to have thoughts other than that of her husband. It was immoral but in light of the previous night, her mind could not be reined in.

Victoria dressed for breakfast in a simple light blue cotton dress. She managed everything before Bea showed up. She helped Lady Victoria with her hair, which she had neatly pulled with small ringlets at the back. She laced up her boots and dabbed on a bit of rose water before she entered the small dining room to join her husband.

"Good Morning Sir" Victoria slipped into a heavy camel chair at the head or the table. She was at one end and Thomas without range of touch at the opposite end.

"My Lady Hawthorne, you must have at least one kiss."

"Why yes sir." Victoria leaned in and gave her husband a peck on the cheek. It was not unlike one she would lay upon her father.

"We shall call on your family before our departure to Burleigh at Devon for our honeymoon trip. It will be a good two weeks of rest before we head to Sherborne House on Nansen Road in London for social season. We will discuss our events further with Martha. She is my secretary and she keeps the social calendar.

"It all sounds fine Lord, but I think I shall have some input on social events while at Sherborne. I am certain Martha is essential at handling the calendar of a bachelor but perhaps not that of a married woman." Lady Victoria suggested.

"Victoria, Martha is worthy; as she was of help to the first Lady Hawthorne and the girls."

"I am not the first Lady Hawthorne. May the dearest June rest in peace. I shall need a personal secretary of my own. I need one who is apprised of the current fashion and protocol. Things change rapidly from season to season. Martha will be necessary to function with you and the others. I shall let Lady Sterling choose for me. She shall be of great assistance while in London. She has done wonders with Persimmon House. She will be among our first visits during social season."

"I see Lady Victoria. The choosing must include Martha as she is of primary importance to my needs. She knows what June and I preferred and she is like a mother to Sophie and Hannah." Victoria grew angry and her voice amplified. This was a change in her. She had become prone to sobbing and feelings of hopelessness.

"Thomas, I am Lady Hawthorne now. Martha is a spinster servant and June, rest her peace, is dead. This is all new to me. You must understand that I cannot live in another's shadow. I respect you as your chosen wife but my needs must be met."

Lord Hawthorne bristled, as his new wife could have been speaking about her physical needs as well. His failure to consummate was a very sensitive subject.

"I will have Martha contact Lady Sterling by proper means. We shall arrange for a private secretary to be at Sherborne House when we arrive to Nansen Court. Do you agree to work with Martha in interim?"

"Yes Lord Hawthorne. I only ask that my status as your wife be recognized in society and…."

"I am aware Victoria. I shall like return of such respect. We will have a pleasant stay at the seashore and deal with matters hence."

Victoria ate her eggs and a sweet meat pie while she sipped her tea.

****

Victoria and Thomas spent two weeks in Southern Britain. Lady Victoria enjoyed the solitude and long walks by the salt marshes and reed beds. She read poetry while Lord Hawthorne poured over his books. He often had his nose in the Bible, although he was not the religious sort. He enjoyed the historical perspective. He would quote scripture in discussion, which would leave other's thinking he was a man of high knowledge. He was a smart man, but hardly worldly. He felt safest in the confines of the island and rarely travelled to the continent.

Lady Victoria was becoming fond of watching migratory birds. She kept a journal of all of her findings. Lord Hawthorne showed no interest in her pursuits and he was hardly able to accompany her on her outings. His feet swelled when he put too much on them.

"We shall head to London day after tomorrow. I have received notes from Lady Elaine and Mother. They will be settling in at Persimmon house with Lady Sterling. I suppose Mary and father will be there also. I cannot wait to settle in at Sherborne. Sophie and Hannah have already made the trip in from Derby Manor. We shall be one large family and surely spoken about highly. I cannot wait to receive callers and the visits will be grand. Oh Thomas, I am so pleased to be presented as Lady Hawthorne." Victoria was beaming from excitement and rosy resulting from recent sunshine.

Victoria had decided, during her walks through the briny spring air, to make the best of a marriage of no love. Lord Hawthorne would have to do. Images of the Duke would occasionally slip in to give her a drop of fantasy. She did not know even his name and probably never would.

****

The trip east was bumpy and lengthy. They spent one overnight in a hotel along the way in Winchester. Lady Victoria enjoyed the stop, as there were shops to accommodate her. She would receive her full wedding trousseau in London. She would need all of the new dresses and jewels, most purchased in Paris, when she and Lord Hawthorne received their first callers as husband and wife. Many things within the trunk had been procured for years as she prepared to enter society as a married lady. She stopped in at Dellie's dress shop to see the offerings.

Victoria had heard good word of them. She had two velvet dresses and two ball gowns with extravagant laces to create elaborate flounces. The colors were mostly shades of green, verdant to olive and in between. Her favorite was made of pink satin with an empire back, bustle and train of fine lace. Her Aunt had sewn pearls into the square neckline.

"Hello. I am Lady Thomas Hawthorne. Your fabrics are lovely. I have heard of your wears and stopped in for a peak. I do not have the time for a proper dress fitting but perhaps you have some bonnets I may see."

"Lady Hawthorne. I am so pleased to be honored with your acquaintance. We heard rumor that you would be for an overnight on your way to Sherborne House. As I said, it was just rumor. I am available to you my Lady. May I prepare you some tea perhaps?" The kind shopkeeper was eager.

"No thank you. I am just weary from travel and thought I might find something to suit my fancy."

Victoria left Dellie's with yards of velvet ribbon and some loose glass beads for the tailor to embellish some of her dresses. She was pleased by the attention she received. She was a woman now, at least in the eyes of society, and she loved it.

****

The carriage entered the city of London at mid-day. Sherborne House was located near the center of town but had grounds to protect its privacy. The energy of the city in June was palpable. Lord Hawthorne was resting while Lady Victoria took in the grandeur. In the past, she had been a visitor, staying with Lady Sterling. Now she was Lady Hawthorne with status and her own home.

The drive was long and bordered by a box-like hedge. There was a pond in front of the house, where a small family of fowl were swimming about. To the left were a series of small out buildings, one that served as a stable. They included a gardening shed, dairy and servant quarters. On the far side of the pond sat a red boathouse and a small dock.

The house came to view as the carriage reached the end of the drive. Victoria's breath was taken away by the grandeur and cleanliness of her new house. The grounds were immaculate with trimmed grass and a rose garden showing red, yellow and perfect blush varieties. The white veranda was climbing with mature wisteria and honeysuckle. Forget fragrance she thought, this could not be bottled.

The home's roof was low pitched and covered in slate. It led to ornate cornices supporting the roof to a wraparound porch, half of which was screened. On top was a cupola that had a scene of the entire property. The doors were black mahogany with substantial brass knobs and a knocker fashioned in the shape of a rosette.

By now, Victoria was up the stone staircase, past the pillars and through the mahogany doors. She was met by John and three others, whose names did not concern her. Lord Hawthorne followed by several footmen who were hauling carpeted bags. Thomas was still drowsy from his nap and he grabbed a spirit from a silver dish James was holding out right.

Lady Victoria entered the parlor out of the grand hallway. The room was warmed by a colossal fireplace. It was made of Italian marble veined in ashen swirls. The furniture in the room was more formal than she become accustomed to at Markham. The couch was deep pink, almost magenta with walnut legs that were arched perfectly. There were matching pillows with gold ornamentation. Three chairs with arms surrounded the couch. A low walnut table ornately carved separated them.

There were small tables on either side of the couch topped in marble. Again, Victoria assumed it was imported from Italy. She stood upon a rug of rich green and crimson. The design was so ornate her vision became dizzy.

The walls were covered except for massive floor to ceiling sash windows. There were curtains of deep green, which were pulled back. One wall held a tapestry that dominated the room imported from the Far East. Other walls held all types of portraits showing gay celebration. There were several gold-flecked frames holding mirrors, which made the parlor look larger than it was.

"Lady would you like a proper tour of the remainder of the house?" James said to Lady Victoria, as she found herself speechless.

"I would like to visit my quarters next. I am tired from the journey."

"Certainly Lady. Please let me introduce you to the housekeeper her at Sherborne. This is Mavis."

"Hello Mavis. I should like some tea in my room before I rest. Any herbal variety will serve."

"Yes, of course my Lady. Welcome to Sherborne. You have a sitting room in your quarters, which has been accommodated to meet your needs by your personal secretary, Blanche. She has arranged all your correspondence for you. The courier has been quite occupied. Your maid will be at your call. The bell sits at your desk and another at your bedside."

"Thank you Mavis. You will take me to by room please." Victoria was weary.

"I shall see you at dinner my lady." Lord Hawthorne remarked as she walked out.

****

Victoria returned to her room and fell into her opulent bed, which had been suited to her desires. All of the pillows were ample and freshly puffed. Her sheets were imported cotton and the blankets were plentiful. Victoria was lost in the comfort and worried not of her tea which was of course delivered as requested.

Could life be any more ideal and lonely at the same point? She mused as she fell into a deep slumber

****

"My Lady we shall have little time to get you refreshed for dinner. Wake up my peach." It was Esther!

"Esther, I knew to expect you at Derby Manor upon return to the country but I did not know if you would arrive here. Oh, me mum. I have not a soul. I wish to tell you everything. It has been such a flurry since I left the estate. The reception, the wedding night, the stay at Devon, Winchester and this grand house. I went to rest hoping for a miracle of companionship and here you stand. It is as if I am back home again." Victoria bounced on the bed.

"It is wonderful to see you well my Lady. You must realize that you are home my love. That door opposite opens to that of you husband. You are Lady Hawthorne. I am your maid. I am happy for that but you must take notice of your husband." Esther spoke as she prepared a new set of clothes for Victoria. She had removed a black satin dress for dinner. With corset ready and camisole next she would make Victoria appropriate for her first meal at Sherborne.

"There is nothing to tell about the Lord. He is but an old man who drinks and smokes his cigars. He is still married to Lady June, may she rest in peace."

"But an heir my Lady. The ghost of his departed Lady June, may she rest in peace, cannot give him that." Esther laced Victoria's corset.

"He slobbered on my bosom. That is all. I remain intact." Victoria wept. Letting go of the tears she dare not show anyone else.

"There, there Victoria. It will take time. You shall not give up. It should only take once, as you are young and healthy. It is truly your duty as a married woman. You shan't lock that door between you and Lord Hawthorne."

"I shall try Esther but I find myself so busied as lady of such a fine house. Esther, this neck has been amended, has it not? I do not recall it dipping so low" Victoria commented as she put on a jewel beaded crimson necklace.

"He will notice. Give it time."

****

Dinner would be held in the formal dining room. It was a long angular table with ornately carved chairs. The sideboard showed a pheasant with root vegetables. Condiments were plentiful as were many breads. Each setting included a chalice for wine. Victoria decided she would partake this evening to calm her feelings.

Joining Thomas and Victoria were Ladies Sophie and Hannah, which would be delightful. Victoria had tired of telling stories that her husband had no concern for.

"Welcome Victoria." Hannah who was the younger girl. She was 18. Chirped.

"Thank you Hannah. It is nice to see you and your sister have taken the journey well."

"We arrived about one hour past you. We had time to settle into our quarters and rest from the journey from Kent." Sophie was louder than Hannah was. She was in her early twenties and a homely girl. She would require arrangements soon or she was at risk of being a spinster.

"Your father and I had a lovely trip to Budleigh at Devon. I shall begin receiving in two days hence. I received word from the Countess that she will be by my side. Of course Lord Hawthorne will join to be accepted as man and wife."

"I will be present my Lady. Just as I did with the first Lady Hawthorne." Thomas spoke.

"Well then, tomorrow we shall take a stroll through the city of London." Hannah announced.

"Brilliant idea sister. It should be a lovely day for a stroll. I will need to stop at the apothecary for some supplies from the chemist. I will have Mavis alert the staff of our intentions."

"It sounds great ladies. I have last been through the streets last season when I was just a girl. Thank you for the opportunity." Victoria was pleased to be invited for a jaunt.

After dinner, they had a glass of sherry and all departed for their quarters. Lord Hawthorne expressed an interest in her décolletage but his glare was not accompanied by any handling.

****

The ladies meandered through the gardens by the palace. The people had come out of the shadows to enjoy a beautiful day. The sun was bold and the ladies were shaded with parasols. They stopped by the apothecary where Sophie picked up some creams for her skin condition. The subject was delicate and they let her enter alone. Victoria eyed an ice cream shop down the street, which she thought delightful.

"Hannah, I would like a vanilla ice cream at the creamery down the street. Will you join me?"

"I do not favor ice cream Lady Victoria. Go ahead and I shall wait here with Constance.

Sophie will join us soon. We will remain here until your return."

"I shall be quick."

Victoria confidently strode to the shop. She reached for the steel doorknob.

"My Lady Hawthorne, allow me."

"Thank you…"

"Duke Jonathan of Wellington. I was at your wedding ceremony to Lord Hawthorne at your father's estate." He spoke and gently took her hand away from the knob and lifted it to his lips. "I was hoping to make your acquaintance. I did not have the time to offer my congratulations at the ceremony."

"Thank you for remembering the event. I appreciate your kind thoughts."

"You were not a vision to forget with your crown of roses and sparkling blue eyes. I hope to see you and Lord Hawthorne this season, as I surely will."

"Yes, I am sure it will be. It was my pleasure to speak with you Sir Duke."

"Jonathan please. Victoria."

With a tip of his top hat, Duke Wellington was gone. So was any thought of ice cream. Victoria floated back to meet the ladies. Her dream had a name and a voice.

CHAPTER SIX

A wrap on the door connecting her room to her husbands alerted Victoria that it was morning. She had never known Lord Hawthorne to enter her quarters and he was never up so early. She still had her sleeping dress and nightcap on. He had certainly not seen her in such a state.

"Come in Thomas" Victoria took off her nightcap quickly.

"Hello Victoria. It is good to see you well. I hear you stirring at dawn on most days. I became concerned and wanted to check on my wife. Your surroundings are beautiful, as they should be. I have never entered your space, I hope you are not offended by my entry." Lord Hawthorne spoke with genuine concern and courtesy.

"Oh no my Lord. You are always welcome. I am your wife and the door is always unlocked for your entry. Thomas, you need not worry. I am not with a lover. I would never do so, as it is not within my character."

Victoria was sitting upright by now and she realized by the light beneath the drapes that she had surely slept beyond her appointed time. Her hair was without its normal style and allowed to cascade down her back. Her head began to ache. She did not know if it was the surprise of having her husband before her while she was unprepared or something else.

"Thomas I am feeling unwell and I have no reason. Perhaps it was the sunshine yesterday that my body was unaccustomed to." Victoria made no movement towards leaving her nest. She was indeed having a spell of some sort.

"My Lady you are without color. Let me feel you." Thomas gently put his palm to young Victoria's forehead. It was a kind, almost fatherly touch. He frowned. "Victoria you are warm. Surely, it was the sun and the exertion of the stroll that has made you ill. Countess Tompkins and Elaine are to be present for breakfast, which you will surely miss. The girls and I will explain your absence. I will notify Esther and Mavis of your condition and they will get you whatever you require. We receive our first callers today and if needed I will receive on our behalf with proper excuses. You rest sweet lady."

Victoria was touched by Lord Hawthorne's manner. She would gladly miss breakfast but a good rest should prepare her for visitors beyond then.

"Thank you Thomas. I need the extra sleep. It seems as if there was another purpose for your visit. You may speak sir if it is an urgent matter." Victoria queried.

"I will speak my words when you are physically at peace. We must allow your body to be well. I will watch over you. You are my wife and this is where I shall remain."

"Thank you my Lord. Rest is all I require. Now you go and explain my absence to Mother and Elaine. I would like word on Mary's whereabouts, as I have received no word from her or about her in some time."

"I will take care of all Victoria." With that, Lord Hawthorne left to take care of matters and enjoy breakfast with the Tompkins ladies.

****

"Good morning Countess, Lady Elaine, ladies."

"Good morning Lord Hawthorne. We were just admiring your fine house here at Nansen Court. Is my daughter, the Lady of the house, going to join us for breakfast?"

"She will not Countess. Lady Hawthorne has taken down with a headache due to too much exertion while in London yesterday. A doctor is not needed and a little extra rest will do her fine. She wishes to receive callers who want to congratulate us on our recent wedding. It will happen as she and Blanche have arranged." Lord Hawthorne announced.

"We understand Lord Hawthorne. The sun yesterday was a shock to her system." Added her sister Lady Elaine.

Lord Hawthorne knew that they imagined she could already be with child, although he knew it was an impossibility. An explanation of the truth would be embarrassing and inappropriate. Eggs, pheasant pie, toast and jam were served, accompanied by some black tea with milk. The room was quiet. Glances were exchanged by the women present. In a way, this was an ongoing conversation. Thoughts were exchanged with no noise. It was proper and secretive.

"My dear son. We have some news we wanted to share with both you and Victoria. I am thinking this way is more appropriate. Victoria will need your comfort and you can prepare yourself. Our cherished Mary has come down with consumption. She has been ill since after your wedding reception and there is no recovery expected. Mary is under a very fine doctor's care and poor Earl Tompkins will not leave the girl's bedside. We have kept word private. We want Victoria and Peter to carry on with their exciting path towards adult life."

"I am in astonishment Countess Maria. This will be of great concern to Lady Hawthorne. She inquired about sweet Mary just today. She will postpone all for her sister."

"Lord Hawthorne, If I may speak on dear Mary's behalf, she would love Victoria to enjoy her entrance into society. She knows things that we do not. She always has and we have joked her about it our whole lives. I have a terrible time explaining this but truly

– she sees great happiness in Victoria's days ahead. She has thought so since the night of the wedding. It must be her future with you Lord Hawthorne. Please do not let the days or weeks ahead be marred for Victoria." Elaine fought back tears. Sophie, the least fair was the first one to take charge of the matters at hand.

"I am deeply changed with sorrow over Mary's condition. We Hawthorne's are strong as are you, the Tompkins's. We have been through a loss with our dear June, may she rest in peace. We must make all happen and we will. We have enough staff to take care of Mary and meet all societal needs. She can be made very comfortable here at Sherborne House." Sophie spoke.

"My dear Lady Sophie, your words touch my heart." The Countess continued. "Mary is resting in comfort at Persimmon House. It is a second home to her and her cousins Sarah and Diana are of great help. She also has the Earl and visits from Peter, although he is taken with plans for his wedding to the Honorable Jane Marley. A move is not necessary at this point, we have alerted Father Cecil from Dover and he will come soon to provide counsel. We have more than enough assistance. Please just take care of Lady Hawthorne. It is to be a time of joy for you and her, as a married couple."

Lord Hawthorne took a breath before speaking. "I will honor your wishes Countess. I will provide Victoria with comfort, as she requires it and make sure she has the joy she deserves. Now my ladies I think we should eat before the feast before us grows cold. John!" John appeared with a glass for Lord Hawthorne.

****

Victoria was well by mid-day and dressed to meet the Countess and Lady Elaine in the parlor with Lord Hawthorne. She dressed in her favored attire of a foam green dress showing a back of intricate brocade detail and a dramatic bustle. The neckline was square. She had grown tired of high-laced necklines and dared to show more flesh. Thomas noticed that portion of her form. She was happy to make him proud. He only gazed and it flattered her. Victoria was growing confidence and it suited her.

"You are ready Lady Hawthorne?"

"I am Lord Hawthorne. We are to receive Lord and Lady Marshall of Surrey. They are a grand couple. They annually have one of the finest events of the season. I dare wish we would receive an invite. They are dear friends of Mother and Father with many children flung allow over. They have a son who has made it to America where he is said to be very prosperous." Victoria was clearly excited by the prospects ahead. Lord Hawthorne had decided to share news of Mary's fragile health that evening.

"You look beautiful Victoria" He glared at her bust with onyx broach.

"Your eyes Lord always slip beneath my speaking mouth." Lady Hawthorne smiled. It had become an innocent joke the pair shared.

"I may be an old man but I can appreciate beauty my dear"

Elaine was fussing on her needlework and the Countess was sipping tea when Lord and Lady Hawthorne joined them in the parlor. A quick nod alerted Elaine and her mother that he had not yet told Victoria of Mary's consumption. Victoria and Thomas sat next to each other on the couch. He appropriately laid his hand over hers. It was the most touch they had shared since their wedding night when Lord Hawthorne had fumbled with her garment. It was never to go any further but it would remain a secret between the two – for now.

****

"Lord and Lady Charles Marshall of Surrey" John announced their guests. They took seats across from the married couple. Mavis served them tea and offered them sweets.

Lady Marshall spoke first. "I am so pleased to visit here at Sherborne. It is one of my favorite homes in all of London. The first Lady Hawthorne left her touch." Lady Marshall knew immediately that she spoke poorly.

"Thank you Lady Marshall, Victoria has her own superb taste she will bring to Nansen Court." Lord Hawthorne provided a save for the visitor.

"Oh yes Lady Hawthorne. I can see immediately that you have distinctive taste. I have never seen beautiful floral arrangements as the ones you display. Please let us dispense with formalities as we are of the same standing. Bess please"

"I shall try Bess. It is a result of my upbringing to use formalities. I suppose it is habit."

"You were raised well." Lord Marshall added with a look towards the Countess.

"We have brought our fondest wishes to you Lord and Lady, but most importantly we wanted to personally deliver invitation to our dance at our home in Chelsea. It will be a formal affair. Details will follow by courier. It will be in three Fridays from now. We hope your calendar allows for your attendance. It goes without mention that Earl Tompkins and the Countess will be invited and Mary, Elaine and Peter as well."

Victoria tried to hide her excitement at being invited to her first formal affair since becoming Lady Hawthorne. "I am certain our schedule can accommodate your affair. I will have my secretary Blanche keep an eye open for the official invitation and reply per instructions."

"I think that is fine. I think we have spoken all of our necessary business. Louis, will you join me in the billiards room?"

"I would be pleased to leave the women to talk fashionable dress and all matter of things."

****

The afternoon progressed smoothly. Victoria and Thomas had a nice meal afterwards. Victoria went on discussing the day's events. She was in an excellent mood. She was beginning to view him as a partner, more of an older brother than husband. It was safe. It was not something causing worry. She had her minor flirtation with the Duke of Wellington to keep her heart aflutter. That was innocent and from afar, it could cause no injury. They had a sip of absinth together in the drawing room when Lord Hawthorne grew dour.

"What is the sudden change in your disposition my Lord?

"I need to speak with you regarding the breakfast you missed with the Countess and the ladies. We spoke of a matter of importance. It concerns your sister Mary."

"I know I missed her 17th birthday but we were at Budleigh and Esther was to deliver a gift in my name. I heard no reply. Is she insulted?"

"No Victoria. Lady Mary has come down with consumption and there is little hope for recovery. She is at Persimmon House with your father by her side."

"Our Mary. The very sweetest of all. She has not an enemy. My dear sister. I must arrange to be at her side my Lord."

"There will be a carriage here in the morning for your transit. I shall accompany you to Persimmon House. Blanche and Martha will handle your social calendar. Mary is resting comfortably under her physician's supervision."

"We need better physicians. Money is of no concern. Father is well and so are we. We can summon the best from across the globe."

"We will help of course my Lady. Father Cecil is on his way from Dover."

Mary was a middle child as Victoria. They shared a like position within the sibling family and always looked after one another.

Victoria took a giant sip of absinthe, in the hopes of getting a little sleep before she went to Persimmon House in the morning. Lord Hawthorne escorted her back to her room and with a peck on the cheek sent his broken wife to bed.

****

"Good Morning father." Lady Hawthorne was escorted into the parlor at Persimmon House. She was met with embrace. Peter and Jane were present as was the rest of the family and others she did not know. "I need to see my sister right away." Victoria was urgent in her request.

"You may Victoria. Father Cecil is with her now and she is saying her peace with God. As soon as he is through you may go in and see Mary. Today will be the day. Before night falls is when the physician says Mary will leave us."

Victoria waited for Father to come out and entered Lady Mary's room. It smelled distinctly different. A mix of Myrrh and death. An odd scent.

"Hello my sister. My sweet Mary. I would have come sooner but was only told last evening. I am so sorry. I wish it were me in your place."

"Victoria it is my time to go and be with our heavenly father. Think of me while riding along the mysterious cliffs of Dover. I shall be within the most spirited mare Benjamin dare saddle. I see things more clearly than ever. You will be happy with child. Your son and your beloved are to be together. Remember our last journey? You must ride with them together and laugh. Teach your boy to laugh. I love you Victoria."

Lady Victoria felt her sister slip away and turn cold to her touch.

She and the family would grieve and spend the next week arranging to have Mary buried at the estate. It was in a plot overlooking the wild hills with lavender allowed to grow thick and unmanaged. Father Cecil performed the ceremony.

It had taken a week to travel back and forth to Dover. The wake was at Markham. Victoria returned to Sherborne exhausted. Lord Hawthorne had been of tremendous help. He cared for Victoria at her most vulnerable and she appreciated the gesture.

Victoria never told another person about Mary's final words. Others would think it was hallucination. Victoria would keep it hers to make sense of someday.

****

Chester House in the center of London was the home of Duke Jonathan Wellington. He stayed at the home during social season with his sister Lady Elizabeth. She was a spinster who devoted herself to the happiness of her brother Jonathan. Both of their parents were deceased and they were the only family they had ever known. They had title and money, which was enough to keep them happy. She was born to serve Jonathan and he was born to be with just about any woman in society.

The Duke was gifted with handsome features and learned excellent manners. He was a well-travelled man and rumored to have left a princess with a broken heart in Paris and one in Switzerland and so on. The Duke loved his sister. He felt responsible for her unmarried status, as she never had time to attract a mate. He always turned to Elizabeth when advice was needed. He trusted his Butler Oliver as well. He did not have a large staff in his cavernous home. He was slow to let outsiders into his life and it had served him well so far.

"Ellie, are you to escort me to the dance at Marshall House on Friday?"

"Yes brother. You really must get a secretary for the few months you are here in London. Your schedule is an untimely mess. I may not always be here to point you in the right direction."

"Lady Elizabeth, you will always be at my side. Where would you go?" Jonathan pecked his sister goodbye and went for a jaunt into town.

****

Victoria was ready to put on her dress for Lord and Lady Marshall's dance at their home in Chelsea. She was excited to step out into society as a married woman. She had been delayed by Mary's death and this would be her first event in formal attire. She would wear an onyx cameo and black earrings as mourning while her Mother would observe by wearing total black. The rules were standard when a spouse was involved but more open when it was a sibling or Daughter.

"Esther is time to strap me into this thing. I want my waist to be less than 27 inches around to accentuate my breast. It will be dramatic with a full effect in back. My dress will present a gracious silhouette. My pearl slippers will peak from beneath. Surely, no one shall see my stockings they are quite delicate with embroidery of rose flowers. They are for my delight only."

"Lady Victoria, perhaps your husband might enjoy your hosiery."

"Esther, Lord Hawthorne is not that way with me. He enjoys his wife in lovely things but he does not touch. No one does. I am like a piece of fine china or a specimen under glass. It is the way it shall be. I will be able to get through one social season before talk begins that I am barren. Lord Hawthorne will decide what story to tell when it becomes necessary."

"You are playing a game of risk my Lady. You are a virgin bride. What if a man comes along to notice you?" Esther was concerned.

"I have risk with a little flirtation I have developed for the Duke of Wellington. He kissed my hand Esther. As a result I am in no way in danger."

"Oh Lady, the Duke of Wellington is a scab. He is known by all of the ladies. Love is just a parlor game to the man."

"He is handsome Esther. I care about little else."

Victoria was cinched in at the waist and she stepped into her pink silk gown. London could be smoggy so light colors were not favored but Lady Victoria liked to be noticed. The neckline was daring and the tailor had surrounded it with the glass beds Victoria purchased in Winchester. Her hair was neatly pulled back to show her ears with gentle tendrils set loose. Her eyes twinkled azure. Her Bosom swelled above her corset. She enhanced the look with sleeves that pulled down over her arms.

"I am prepared Esther. Is my husband waiting in the foyer?"

"He is, my beautiful Lady."

****

"Lord and Lady Thomas Hawthorne"

Victoria and Thomas entered the formal hall at the Marshall's home. Victoria stood out in her unique costume and Thomas looked fine in his black three- piece suit and top hat. There was a string company playing delightful music. Thomas took his wife in his arms and danced with agility. Victoria was impressed, as he was not always steady on his feet. Lady Hawthorne was light as air and Thomas knew she stood out for her beauty. They took a break to sip champagne and socialize with others.

"Lady Hawthorne." A gloved hand appeared out of nowhere. "Will you give me the pleasure of dancing with you? I am Jonathan, Duke of Wellington. We met weeks back in the London streets."

"Yes. I remember you and you may have this dance." Lord Hawthorne gestured his approval.

Lady Hawthorne felt very safe and much unmarried in the Duke's hands. He was a skilled dancer. He held his lead firmly but enjoyed letting the Lady push a bit. It felt natural. They were as one on the dance floor.

"Lady Hawthorne I am impressed you recall our meeting. It was brief. I wished to engage you further but an ice cream shop did not make an appropriate place."

"I am a married woman Sir. I do not think there was an appropriate place"

"Lady, you assume I was suggesting something torrid. Assumptions can be dangerous."

"I have been warned of you Duke of Wellington. I am not one to engage in folly."

"Be warned Victoria."

"We talk too much in this dance. I am Lady Hawthorne hence forth."

"Let it be so Victoria, I am to be called Jonathan. Does your new husband approve of your show of skin?" Jonathan's smile curled as he waited for a response. "You have no return of my comment my Lady?"

"I am without words. You are flirting with a married woman."

"A beautiful married woman and too young to be wed to an old man."

"I do think the music has gone quiet. Thank you for the dance Sir Jonathan and the intriguing conversation. Please escort me back to my husband."

Victoria returned to Lord Hawthorne, hot from the encounter with the Duke. They walked across the floor to refill their glasses. Jonathan tracked Victoria with his eyes. She could feel his gaze.

****

The Duke took a carriage home with Elizabeth. It was not his usual custom to return home with his sister.

"Is there trouble with you Jonathan? You seem out of sorts and you never return to the house with me. I do not recall a time you have left without a conquest."

"Dear Sister I have a new challenge. I am to begin courtship of a married lady. It is a game I have not played before. She is not available to me and she interests me. I will need your aid and discretion with this matter. I will start by sending her letters penned from my hand and personally delivered. You will assist with this matter. Are you game?"

"Dear Jonathan, it is without taste. What of the husband?"

"He is but an old man. I will be a gift to Lady Victoria." The Duke smiled.

"Lady Hawthorne? Oh Jonathan. She is daughter of Earl Tompkins of Markham. They just buried a daughter. The Hawthorne's are too respected to play games among."

"I cannot be without Lady Hawthorne. Your aide?"

"I cannot say no to you brother."

****

Lady Hawthorne and her husband returned to Sherborne. They were exhausted after a full night of dancing. Thomas would need a hot bath with salts to ease his swelling.

"You looked lovely tonight Victoria. It was not wasted on me. Your beauty enchanted all of the gentlemen present. You were dazzling. Please do not make a mockery of my name. My reputation is very urgent to me. Please give me your honor as Lady Hawthorne, my wife."

Victoria began to sweat from her brow. She relived her dance with the Duke of Wellington time after time. She had to believe it was harmless flirtation. She was beginning to appreciate Thomas and respect him.

"I promise to honor you Lord Hawthorne, my husband."

CHAPTER SEVEN

Victoria was the first thing on Jonathan's mind as he got out of bed. He had surprised himself by dreaming of her as he slept. Her scent was floral but he could not identify it. He knew it would become something he would come to identify with his Victoria. She carried herself with confidence, as she had been raised in a family with flawless etiquette. Jonathan was nearly giddy with excitement at the journey ahead. He had never courted a married lady and the threat of discovery made the romance dangerous. He became flushed at what might come.

He thought putting pen to paper was a way he could covertly convey his feelings to Lady Hawthorne. He would need fresh sheets of paper and a sturdy pen with a supply of ink, black to make his statement bold. His sister made mention of his lack of a formal secretary, that was true, so he had to procure supplies through Elizabeth and Oliver. Oliver might as well have a line of buttons for a mouth. He never opened it where Jonathan was concerned. He was known, however for rolling his eyes. The Duke of Wellington earned countless eye rolls. The new mission of his would cause his trusted butler to have an aching head.

"Good morning Lady Elizabeth." Jonathan gave his sister a gentile kiss on the cheek. "You look well. I would not guess you were awake when the time struck midnight. You were travelling home with me so I know you were alert. Do you recall my request of your partnership in my new appropriation?"

"I do Jonathan. I hoped you would wake with better sense."

"No my Lady. I am to proceed enthusiastically with your help. I will have assignments for Oliver as well. I am sure you spend many hours alone in you room reading poet's work. I should need access to you readings. We shall begin with a simple note first, in which I express my intentions. Later I plan to include quotations from the finest writers. We can begin with the obvious – Lord Byron. I may even try my skills and create a poem of my own words.

"It sounds like my little brother may be looking for something to occupy his time. I wonder Jonathan, if you have not considered the breakable heart of young Victoria."

"Elizabeth, the sharing of my feelings will be a fair game between Lady Hawthorne and myself. A lady of almost 18 and a man over 60 years of age is hideous. I am presenting my lady with temporary relief from a mundane life. We shall explore the bedroom together and then I shall release her back to Lord Hawthorne." The Duke smiled at his neat explanation of the matter.

"Sir, Lady Elizabeth, I do not intend to interrupt but I am inquiring about your needs of the day. Do I need to arrange for a carriage?" It was customary for Oliver to allow the brother and sister time to chat before he put plans for the day in place.

Lady Elizabeth adjusted her demeanor when Oliver entered the dining room. Oliver was early in his 50's. He had known the parents of the Duke and his sister. He was a father figure to both of them. He always knew he was a butler and followed formal protocol but all knew he was more of a family member than anything else.

"Oliver, the Duke was just filling me in on his new intended and the role we shall both play in the adventure." Elizabeth welcomed Oliver into the conversation.

"This is the first I have heard of said adventure."

"Oh my dear butler, when have you ever been the last to know anything. Your ears work very well behind closed doors." Jonathan laughed.

"What can I perform for you sir?" Oliver was unsuccessful at seeming unaware of the matter.

"I will need supplies for writing letters; most importantly I need a new seal and wax scented in musk. I need a length of crimson silk fabric. I will require one single pearl that can be secured to such cloth."

"Consider it done by sundown. The paper?" Oliver inquired.

"It should be heavy ivory colored parchment. The very highest of quality but discreet. My seal shall identify me personally. A simple R will do. Wax should be sapphire blue resembling my Lady's eyes." Jonathan sighed.

"How do you plan to get the notes delivered brother?"

"It is social season and Lady Hawthorne is to have many visits by courier. Her secretary will intercept them. We shall employ our own such person, as the secretary is probably newly hired. We must find someone Lady trusts implicitly."

"Would you like me to inquire? This person most likely exists. I will pay a visit to Persimmon House to offer my condolences on the recent passing of Lady Mary Tompkins, may she rest in peace. I will be able to inquire about life at Sherborne."

"I like your ideas Ellie. You are a great benefit. It is going to be as a caper. The very mystery causes my hairs to stand."

"Oliver, I will arrange to make a call to Persimmon House. You will make sure I have a carriage at my disposal?"

"Of course Elizabeth. I meant Lady. Excuse my lapse." Oliver turned color and Elizabeth blushed as well. They shared a glance.

The Duke of Wellington retreated to his study. He was to practice his hand. He was not accustomed courting a lady through letters. He was happy to begin his plan.

****

"Good morning Esther. I am to spend some hours at my desk this morning before I receive guests. My sister Elaine is going to be over to join me. We shall visit with the Tully's for most of the afternoon. They wish to extend their condolences and best wishes. I am unsure which these days. It is most confusing and I wish I had dear Mary to provide me wisdom." Victoria sighed as she departed Esther's company.

Victoria did not mention her dance with the Duke of Wellington. It was breaking laws of etiquette and she was disconcerted. She had made a promise to Lord Hawthorne. She would not shame his well-preserved name. She had but one short dance with the Duke; certainly, she could expect nothing more. Her last view of him was his focused eyes. They had seared him in Victoria's memory, but that is how it would remain. A memory.

****

"May I interrupt you Lady Hawthorne?" Esther cautiously approached.

"Yes of course Esther. I am sorry if I was terse when we spoke last. I am tired from the demands upon me as of late."

"I have received a note from a courier that is to be delivered to you only. It did not come by post. Strict instructions led me to you and told me not to include Blanche in the duty. It is very odd Victoria. I have not laid eyes on the gentleman courier before." Esther seemed perplexed.

"Thank you Esther. I am also curious. You may leave the note with me. It is someone being clever to assure that I will read the missive. I will let you know if I need your further assistance. Thank you Esther."

The seal was a unique shade of blue, as she had never seen before. A wax seal with a hint of fragrance showed a simple "J". It was addressed only to "Victoria". The ink was fresh. Lady Hawthorne's palms became dewy as she broke the seal

> *Dearest Victoria:*
>
> *Please accept my forgiveness for presuming to pen you a note. I reveal my intentions towards you because the choice is not mine. I am driven*

by my heart. Your beauty grows each time I am in the honor of your presence. Your delicate features and confidence have shown since I first laid eyes upon you. You were all in white with a crown of roses. You were given to not only your husband on that day but unto me. A stranger in a crimson tide.

Please accept my feelings through your pen. The exchange is to be trusted.

Jonathan

A small red piece of red silk with a single pearl fell from the note. Victoria's spirits rose beyond anything she had before felt. She felt as she belonged to someone. It was not similar to the contract she shared with Thomas. He had never physically changed her composure through a note or other means. She got out her writing essentials at once. Her hand was trembling, but as Jonathan had done, she would let her heart lead.

Dear Jonathan:

I received your letter of intentions. My feelings of our meeting on the streets of London and our Dance at Lord and Lady Marshall's home were discovered the night we shared our first glance. I am pleased you also share the memory. I too am driven by my heart.

Victoria

Victoria sealed it with a letter "H" with lavender wax. She would have preferred a "V" but did not have one available. Her recent scent was lily of the valley she had imported from America. She had decided on the scent only recently because it made her stand apart from the others. She put a light dab upon the note.

"Esther I need you to find the new courier you spoke of and return this immediately. Your discretion is required. Do not allow the Lord to know of your actions." The urgency in Victoria's tone was new to Esther. She looked concerned.

"You have my absolute care. You know that Lady, but are you certain of your actions?"

"Yes Esther. It is indeed the Duke of Wellington as I know you suspect. I never knew courtship with Lord Hawthorne. This is all quite innocent."

"I will hold my tongue but I have given you warning. I am here to protect you above all else." Esther was stern.

"The courier Esther. Now!"

"Done, Lady Hawthorne."

****

The Duke of Wellington received the note carried by Oliver.

"This arrived by courier this afternoon. It was freshly penned."

The note had the scent he remembered Lady Hawthorne wearing the night of the dance. It was not over-done. Only detected by a nose, which had smelled it before. He opened the note, to find a slip of pink satin. Attached to it was a single blue glass bead.

"Oliver, I need you to arrange a visit to Sherborne House. Lady Elizabeth and I will call on the new Lord and Lady Hawthorne."

"Oliver rolled his eyes."

CHAPTER EIGHT

Blanche approached Lady Hawthorne before breakfast with a schedule of this day's events. It had become routine. She had been insistent about receiving a secretary of her own and Blanche was working out nicely. Victoria had Esther to rely on for the most private matters, as the correspondence from the Duke. It had been over 24 hours since she sent reply. Her mood was buoyant as she waited for another note. It was Monday and she had to keep her busy schedule to warn no one of her secret dalliance.

Victoria sat down at her vanity, waiting for Esther to arrive and arrange her hair. After breakfast and time to rest, she and Lord Hawthorne were in the habit of receiving callers. She began with the names of her guests.

I.   `Duke Jonathan of Wellington and Lady Elizabeth (sister)`

Victoria read no more.

"Blanche, may I see you" Victoria called out.

"Yes Lady Hawthorne. You sound urgent. Are you in physical need my lady?"

Victoria calmed herself before speaking. "No Blanche. There is nothing wrong. I was curious about my first appointment on my schedule. The Duke of Wellington and his sister Elizabeth were a surprise to see."

"Yes Lady Hawthorne. The arrangement was made just last evening. It seems the Tully's were not to be here in time. The Duke and Lady Elizabeth inquired and I thought they were a suitable pair to fill the gap. They know of your recent loss and since they live here in London, they wanted to avail themselves to you and Lord Hawthorne. Is there some discomfort you have in receiving them?"

"Certainly not Blanche. I had expected to see the Tully's and you have explained all. Please have Esther come at once. I have soiled my olive dress and prefer a different one."

****

"I will see you at noon for our ride to Sherborne. I trust you are aware our plans for a visit."

"I am brother. You cannot be up to good things with this game you have created. We are to call on Lady Hawthorne with the Lord present? I will be your consort in this but I do not aid willingly."

"Ellie, you fret too much. I am skilled at being the most proper caller. I will enjoy my time with both the Lord and Lady. Shall be fun to witness I should think. Oliver? I sense you are listening nearby and you can enter now with my kipper and ham. I am ravenous. This Lady Hawthorne has stimulated my appetite. I am hungry too." Lord Wellington was excessively jovial.

"Jonathan, may I lay out your usual black coat and pants?" Oliver asked.

"Yes Oliver. I wish to include the white shirt I recently received from Milan and one single pearl pin for my lapel. I should appear proper yet hopeful. Not ordinary."

"Jonathan, ordinary is not part of your make-up." Elizabeth added.

****

"May I introduce Jonathan, Duke of Wellington and Lady Elizabeth."

Victoria sat statuesque next to Lord Hawthorne. She was wearing a light peach dress, which was abundant with many layers of tulle creating a full effect. Her tiny waist gave way to her creamy bust. The weather was warm so she was free to wear short sleeves. She wore diamonds on her neck and in her ears. Her hair was pulled back and over her ears. It was more bouffant than she had worn it before. She had become more daring in her choice of style.

Jonathan noticed her choice of dress and the change since less than one week prior. Lady Hawthorne held her husband's hand with pride. She was comfortable holding court in her finely appointed parlor.

"Are you just in London for the season Sir? Where do you spend the remainder of your time? I know you were present at our wedding reception but I do know your habits." Victoria spoke.

"I have a flat in Paris and a home in Switzerland both of which I visit with my sister and my butler Oliver. Of course, I have a country manor down by Winchester. It is only a day's travel from Derby Manor where you spend your time."

"We shall be as neighbors. We will visit at holiday time." Victoria replied. The two were doing all of the exchange.

"Yes. Elizabeth we must keep Lord and Lady Hawthorne in mind this winter." Jonathan commented.

"Yes Sir. I will do that. Lady Hawthorne you must accept our most sincere sorrow over the death of Lady Mary. Neither my brother nor I were in close association with your sister but she was a lovely girl."

"She resembled you Lady Hawthorne. He complimented Victoria and she noticed while it drifted past the others."

"Well Sir Jonathan, why don't you join me in the drawing room? I would love to hear of your travels to the continent. I am planning to take Lady Hawthorne to Paris."

"The trip will be magnificent. I should think you should schedule it before, well you know." They walked to the drawing room.

Jonathan brushed up against Victoria's dress while exiting. Their eyes momentarily engaged. It was missed by Lady Elizabeth and Lord Hawthorne.

The gentlemen played billiards and drank spirits. Elizabeth and Victoria chatted about fashion and some fabulous scandals that had tongues wagging throughout London. Lady Hawthorne knew the brother and sister were close. She did not imagine Elizabeth was privy to every detail.

"The Duke of Wellington and I have just received an invitation to the ball at Persimmon House week after next. I have sent reply. Your Aunt Lady Sterling always throws the finest occasions. Will we see you and Lord Hawthorne in attendance?"

"I should think so. The Countess Maria, my mother, has been helping plan the ball for months. They have more staff than any event in London. It should be grand. Are you going to bring an escort or will Jonathan, I mean The Duke, serve as such?"

"At a grand affair as Lady Winter's ball we routinely serve as the other's escort. My brother is open to fill his dance card with many women." Elizabeth added, perhaps hoping for reaction.

"I see."

"Perhaps you will share a dance with my brother *again*."

"Let us invite the men to rejoin us." Victoria said hastily.

Lord Hawthorne and the Duke rejoined the group and exchanged pleasant farewells.

"Thank you Lady Hawthorne for having my sister and me as guests. We should like to return the pleasantry in our London home. Sherborne has never looked finer."

With a bow, Jonathan and Elizabeth took to their carriage. Victoria's demeanor appeared unchanged but inside she was as a child at Christmas waiting to open gifts. She would expect a note soon.

****

Dearest Victoria:

My pen quivers in my hand. I was enchanted by your presence at Sherborne House. The space between us today was temporary, as

> *we must meet so that I may touch what you possess. My Lord Byron has better words than I do.*
>
> > *And on that Cheek, and o'er that brow,*
> >
> > *So soft, so calm, yet eloquent,*
>
> *I will not continue the words through pen, as I wish to whisper them in your tender ear. Please respond with heart and direction.*
>
> *Jonathan*

Victoria read the note quickly and once more. Slowly the second time so she was able to calm herself before she wrote her reply.

> *Jonathan:*
>
> > *I find it impossible to express myself through written words. I live for your breath upon my ears to hear Lord Byron further. The air tonight is warm and I am tempted to take a stroll on Nansen Court by the boathouse. It is my*

habit to take such strolls. I go unnoticed.

Victoria

"Esther I will enjoy dinner with Lord Hawthorne and the Ladies Sophie and Hannah. After I will take immediately to my quarters. You will assure me when everyone has retreated to the second floor. I will stroll at dark, as I am accustomed to do on occasion. My absence is to be ignored by all. I hope Lord Hawthorne partakes in much gin. You will make certain the night goes without incident."

"I will do as you ask my Lady. Please be cautious. There is little I can do. You are like a boulder rolling down a hill that cannot be stopped. I love you Victoria."

****

Lady Hawthorne excused herself after dinner.

"It was a wonderful meal. I am so pleased to hear of your sketch work Hannah. I will visit your studio tomorrow and inspect your progress. I will not be in the drawing room for sherry tonight. I am tired from an eventful day. You sleep well my Lord. I will see you at breakfast in the morning at ten."

Victoria kissed her husband goodnight and scurried away to her room to dress for her rendezvous with the Duke. Her trousseau included lingerie that she had never dared to wear. She had no occasion to dress for such an occasion but it seemed like the time. She had a corset on already. She had on bloomers, which she replaced with embroidered hosiery and a garter belt. The corset covered her breast to expose her décolletage. She would not cover up with a brassiere. She chose a satin lavender gown that reached her toes and allowed her arms free. She covered up with a white cotton robe and added petite slippers with dainty rosettes. Lilly of the valley and talc powder and she was almost prepared to go. Victoria removed the pins from her hair. No man had ever seen her natural waves as they cascaded down her back.

Victoria tiptoed out of the house and down the stone staircase.

She walked the half mile to the pond. The family of ducks was absent. For a moment, she wondered where they spent their nights.

Did the male and female lay together, as was custom between some married couples. She had never known it to happen but Mary once told her that sweet Benjamin shared a bed with his wife in a tiny house on the estate. He loved that plain old woman who worked in the dairy back home.

Victoria continued to the little red boathouse. She would visit the place often. It was in the trees at the far end of the pond and was easily missed except for its color. She used it as a place to go where she was free to sing rhyming sounds aloud or cry if she needed a release. It had once been a working boathouse. Sculls were stored when the former residents would practice for racing on the Thames. There were some left behind that had grown cracked and covered in moss. Surely they were not worthy for the water still. Two tiny rowboats sat ready to launch. No one at Sherborne seemed interested in taking them out. There was an old butcher-block table and eight stools. Victoria would occasionally find a discarded ale mug laying on top. She assumed it was someone from the stables or dairy who had stolen a break. The out houses were located at the opposite side of the pond so she knew there would be no visitors at night. Beyond that, a family of stray cats would gather in a tiny bunkroom. Victoria brought milk from the dairy for them to lap up, when she thought of it.

The boathouse had no lighting as the main house. There was a cabinet full of candles and lanterns too. Victoria had brought a couple of oil lamps and fuel so she could read. There was no running water but a pump nearby was working if necessary. Some may say it was a ramshackle mess but it was Victoria's to call her own and for that reason, she loved it.

Victoria grew nervous, as she got closer. She knew not what to expect. She was not raised to meet with men other than her husband. Women of a different sort had such assignations. Her dress would surely send Jonathan signals that she should not be sending. Her desires over ruled her fears.

"Victoria. Is that you moving in the shadows?"

"It is I Jonathan. It is my hope that you have not been waiting long on the dock with no lighting."

"The moon and stars provide a tranquil retreat. I have not been here one hour. Come out of the dark Victoria."

Victoria stepped into the moonlight. Jonathan was in his pinstriped pants with a loose muslin top. He wore no tie or jacket.

"I left London as soon as I read your note. I rode my own stead; I could not bear the time it would take to prepare a carriage. My eyes are burning as I look at you now with your long curls and a dress to accentuate the natural curves of your body. I have only dreamed of such ethereal beauty."

Victoria took a breath, as it was all she could manage. Jonathan took Victoria in his arms, a place she had never known. He pulled her in by her hair in a manner that was resolute and gentle at the same moment. The Duke of Wellington kissed Lady Hawthorne firmly on the mouth. She was carried into the boathouse and laid upon the butcher-block table. Victoria, who favored her soft bed and sumptuous puffs, was glad to be without the hindrance of blankets and cushions. Her eyes spoke when her words went silent.

Jonathan gently remove Victoria's white cotton robe and lavender dress. Victoria was bear in her corset and hosiery. A state she had never been seen by a man before. He touched her breast and kissed her body with ease. Jonathan untied her corset and removed her hose one at a time as he kissed his way to her feet. Victoria did not protest.

Jonathan and Victoria made love upon the table.

"I have no words to describe my feelings. I did not have control of my body. I surely did not have control of my mind. It was more than any fantasy could describe." Victoria remarked.

"Victoria, you are my beauty. You are free from your confines now. You are my lover. The pleasure when we meet next will be more intense. It will only grow beyond that. I am discreet and you will remain my secret treasure. When you engage in marital affairs with Lord Hawthorne you will think of me and this magical moment."

Victoria grew silent. There would be no marital affairs. He did not realize she was a virgin. Who would guess?

"I share your thoughts dear Jonathan. I shall think of this time always but perhaps not while I am in the arms of Lord Hawthorne."

"I assumed too much. I am feeling something you are not?" Jonathan spoke with confusion.

"I am yours alone dearest Jonathan. I was never touched by a man until just tonight,"

"Victoria you were a virgin?"

"I performed for you out of passion not out of experience. Lord Hawthorne and I have never consummated our union."

Jonathan spoke." I am astonished. From my own lips, I have warned against assumptions. I should have known. I did not wish to take such a precious thing from you. I would have led you softer and slower as a teacher should. I did not intend to throw you on a table and steal from you."

"You cannot steal what is freely given. I must leave in haste before my absence is noticed."

Lady Hawthorne layered on her dress and cotton robe with her slippers. She grabbed her corset and garter belt. She put her hosiery in Lord Wellington's hands and with a kiss, she was out the door.

Jonathan sat stunned.

CHAPTER NINE

Victoria was awake at dawn. She was quiet, as she did not want to alert Esther. She needed time to relive the previous night. She had to be certain it had really occurred. Her body was sore due to the hard surface of the butcher-block table. She had bruises on her spine that she felt but had not yet viewed in the mirror. She felt changed and she feared she would appear different. It was much to consider. She rolled over and went back to sleep. Under her pillow was pinned her small piece of crimson cloth with a single pearl.

****

The Duke of Hawthorne found himself alone between the pillars in bed. He was not alone, for he slept with clear memory of Victoria. It was perhaps the first time he had been with a virgin. He mused if his actions would have been different if he had known. It was unusual for Jonathan to have lingering feelings for a woman when the lovemaking was finished. He wished to remain in the privacy of his room for a while longer. He recommitted to sleep in the hopes he would dream of his Victoria. He held her hose to his cheek and closed his eyes.

The Duke decided to begin the day. He called his friend.

"Oliver!"

"Good Morning Sir. Did you sleep well? I waited for your return last night. You left in such I hurry that I feared there was something the matter. I see you are awake, but not quite with us yet. I have tea prepared and cook will serve you and Lady Elizabeth breakfast accordingly."

"Thank you Oliver. The courier you have arranged is working out quite nicely. I will have a note that should be sent later this morning. Can you tell me if we still have access to your friends flat on Hingham Road? I will need a pair of access keys brought to my room if it is still available."

"Oh…um yes Sir. I know it is available. I will stock it with necessary provisions and make sure the linens are fresh." Oliver replied and seemed surprised at the request.

"Oliver? Who is the friend of yours? Can I expect the flat available for use?"

"Yes Sir Duke you can expect such. He is a man of odd sorts. He has taken leave to Wales for an extended break."

"That is all I need to know Oliver. Please tell this friend of yours *thank you*." Jonathan ended the subject. He thought for a moment that Oliver might use the space for his own pleasurable trysts. He put the subject out of mind. Oliver would have no time for a lady. He and the spinster Elizabeth constantly occupied him.

"It looks like a nice morning Elizabeth. The moon was shining bright last night providing hope for clear skies today." The Duke of Wellington took his seat across from his sister.

"Dear brother you would know the sky last night. You have taken to star gazing. Is Lady Hawthorne well?" Elizabeth asked.

"Lady Hawthorne is quite well."

"As you said with your own words, you are to return the Lady to her husband. I see a change in you Jonathan that signals that you have showed the Lady the bedroom. Will she be back in the arms of Lord Hawthorne now that your fancy has been fulfilled?"

Elizabeth was direct. She was after all a lady and knew of how deep feelings could run. She worried for Victoria, and how she might be treated by Jonathan who was surely a bon vivant.

"I find myself extending this dalliance with Lady Hawthorne. I am certain she will be amenable to my plans."

"Be careful little brother." Elizabeth warned.

"Oliver? Have you heard all? Come join us." Jonathan called out to the hallway. Where Oliver stood as sentry.

"Sir Jonathan I have the courier at your disposal when you are ready to send a note. I have put the two keys requested in your ivory box atop your changing table."

"Perfect Oliver. From where did the courier come? He is but 15 years old. I trust him but I am curious."

"He is an old cousin. I unofficially apprentice him. He will make a fine butler someday. It shall be in a home even grander than this. That is not to say yours is not grand." Oliver slipped away. His explanation was sufficient.

****

Lady Hawthorne returned to her room after breakfast to find the parchment sealed note on her pillow.

> *My Dear Victoria:*
>
> *My day is like no other. Your sweet smell remains on my clothing and your stockings are my reminder of our evening as lovers. I give you entrance to four Hingham Street. I am bold to request your presence. My sister, the Lady Elizabeth will provide reason for your departure at three in the afternoon.*
>
> *Jonathan*

A black iron key fell to her lap. It was attached to a red ribbon with a single pearl as its anchor. Victoria picked up her fountain pen to reply.

> *My Jonathan:*
>
> *I am blissfully in receipt of your invitation. I will wait for instruction from Lady Elizabeth. I trust thine lady's discretion if you say it is so.*

The moments will appear long until I can be in your arms once again.

Your Victoria

Victoria sealed it with a simple letter "V". She had Esther acquire a new insignia for her personal use.

"Esther, please leave this to the courier who awaits." Victoria had anticipated words. Esther's pursing of her lips said enough.

****

Lady Elaine and Countess Maria joined Lady Hawthorne in the parlor where they were to receive the widowed Baron and his daughters Lady Madeline and Lady Suzanne. Baron Stephan had lost the lovely Baroness when her ferry from France to Great Britain took on water. There were no survivors. He and his daughters had stayed at Markham Estate for six months in the aftermath. The Baron held out hope that his beloved would someday return. He stayed by the White Cliffs of Dover for that reason. Many said that her ghost haunts the Cliffs. It provided endless stories when Victoria was a young girl.

Madeline and Suzanne were like sisters. They would soon become betrothed. Baron Stephan would select carefully for his girls. Madeline would find a husband first as she was 20 and Suzanne was just 17. The Baron would marry again but first he would take care of his girls. There seemed to be a dearth of girls in London that season and a need for male heirs.

"May I announce The Baron Stephan of Hampshire and the Ladies Madeline and Suzanne."

"Baron Stephan you look well. Welcome to Sherborne. Lord Hawthorne is busy with work in London today. He had to handle some financial matters that he could not handle from Nansen Court."

Lady Hawthorne made proper introductions, although they were already in acquaintance. Mavis presented the group with tea and fresh biscuits. Victoria was growing accustomed to visitors and delighted that Sherborne was high on everyone's list of homes to visit. She knew what the afternoon had waiting for her. Her disposition was cheerful.

"Do tell us the events you have upcoming on your calendar." The Countess began.

"We will be attending the ball at Persimmon House." Baron answered, before he was interrupted.

"Of course we will. It will be the event of the season. My sister Madeline is certain to gain attention. She is expected to dance with all of the eligible gentlemen. Are you not sister?"

"Under father's watchful eye. My feet will ache." Madeline answered.

"Are your plans to return to Hampshire after the season Baron?" Victoria questioned.

"Those are my plans Lady Hawthorne. I have personal plans to dedicate my time to until then."

"Well, good enough Baron. We shall be delighted to see you at the ball."

The Baron and his daughters departed after a cordial visit. Countess Maria was pleased with the bits of gossip she received. She would begin thinking of a dashing bachelor for Lady Madeline and the Baron would be soon seeking a young bride to present him an heir. With only four children, she availed herself to all as matchmaker. She found it as a way to occupy time.

Blanche entered the parlor.

"My Ladies, Countess, may I interrupt your conversation. A letter came from The Duke of Wellington's house for Lady Victoria. It was marked to be opened immediately."

Victoria was stunned. Why would Jonathan be so careless? It had not come from the special courier and it was in Blanche's hands. She would certainly inquire why a single man was corresponding with a married lady. She barely retained her composure.

"Please give it to me Blanche." Elaine and her mother were close by.

Victoria opened the note. It was showing a "W" on the seal. Victoria breathed a sigh of relief.

> *Dear Lady Hawthorne:*
>
> *I have a personal matter to discuss with you. It is female in nature and I find myself in a houseful of gentlemen. If you may be of service, I*

can send a carriage for you just before 3pm today. You may stay to enjoy dinner with me as my brother is away on commitments.

Lady Elizabeth

"It is from Lady Elizabeth who needs my assistance today at 3 O'clock. The matter is delicate. Lord Hawthorne is away most of the day so my time allows. I will certainly assist Lady Elizabeth in her time of need. She was so kind to pay her condolences regarding Mary, may she rest in peace."

"Victoria you are a kind friend to Lady Elizabeth. I am sure your husband will stand behind your decision to honor her request."

"Victoria" Elaine chimed in. "I thought you were receiving a note from The Duke. Would not that be a scandal?"

"Lady Elaine, you do have an imagination. I am a married lady" Victoria swallowed hard.

Lady Hawthorne left word for Ladies Sophie and Hannah and handwritten message to her husband. Jonathan had indeed thought of everything. Her absence was explained in front of her mother and sister. He had even thought of transport.

Victoria dressed as she would for a friendly visit. She felt like a character in an espionage story. She wore her sea foam dress with a high lace collar and wide sleeves. Crinolines would add drama and a bustle completed the silhouette. She buttoned up her heeled brown boots in a size six of course. She topped the costume off with a small black hat.

"Esther please come and help me with my buttons. I got most of my self dressed without your aid. I have increased stamina. The buttons in back are an impossibility."

"Lady Hawthorne, we both know Lady Elizabeth has nothing to do with your outing. The wool has been pulled over your husband's eyes this time. What are you doing Victoria? This cannot continue all the while you are in London. Heaven help you should you sleep with the Duke of Wellington. I worry you will become but another of his conquests."

"Too late for worries. I am carrying on an affair with Jonathan. I am more to him than you know. It is destiny Esther. I know not where this shall go. Where he goes I will follow."

"My prayers are with you Victoria. The heart cannot be contained. I may be an old maid but inside I know the strength of such feelings."

"Esther. I understand your concern. Discretion is in the foremost of my mind."

Victoria added a cameo necklace and rubbed some fragrance on her wrists. She waited for Mavis to alert her when the carriage arrived.

****

Jonathan opened the heavy wooden door to the flat on Hingham Street in London. It was a three-bedroom unit with two floors. It was an upper-middle class neighborhood. A place he and Victoria would go unnoticed. It was modestly decorated with a couch and chairs in front of a fireplace made of granite shipped in from Wales. It had gas lighting and a water closet, which made it comfortable. The Duke of Wellington had the highest of standards when it came to accommodations. He considered for a moment that any more comfort was excessive. The thought passed.

Oliver had provided supplies in the kitchen. There was wine in a decanter on the table and fresh fruit and cheese on a platter. There were some lavender jellies on the table nearby. Oliver knew the Duke had a taste for the confections.

Jonathan took off his frock coat and relaxed on the couch. He was remarkably calm. Victoria made him feel safe which is not a feeling he was accustomed. Perhaps he was left feeling ill at ease due to the early passing of his mother and father. Money was always there but he was always seeking his next conquest. Since Victoria, he could easily be just Jonathan, not the Duke of Wellington.

Victoria was at the door.

"May I enter Sir Duke?"

"I know no Duke when I am with you Victoria." Jonathan replied.

"I was unsure about using the key. I was filled with fear that you would not be here."

"I would be nowhere else. I promise someday we will make love in a bed of feathers and the finest linens. This flat does not offer much in the way of comforts."

"I should say Jonathan that it is formal compared to a boathouse with a butcher-block table."

"It has you and that fulfills my every need." Jonathan finished.

Jonathan took off Victoria's hat and released her hair so it flowed like waves down her back. He began the chore of unbuttoning her green dress. He handled her with care. Words went unspoken and she allowed Jonathan to release her from her layers of fabric. When he was done, she performed the same ritual on him. He caressed her body, as she herself had never done, taking time for every curve.

They fell upon the floor in front of the fire and gave into one another.

"Jonathan I feel for you more than yesterday. What comes tomorrow? I do not think my life at Sherborne will ever meet my needs."

"My love, it seems as tears may come. Please do not cloud your beautiful blue eyes."

"Such emotion causes turmoil for I do not know how to reign it back." Victoria fought tears.

"I have something to brighten your spirits." Jonathan revealed a black velvet box. In it were a pair of sapphire earrings. They were simple blue stones matching her eyes.

"Jonathan. They are perfect as you are. I will always cherish them and keep them near."

They had a glass of wine. Their lives were filled with paid staff so it felt liberating to fetch for themselves. In each other's arms, they slept.

"Jonathan wake up you must secure my buttons for me. I am to be late back to Nansen Court. The sun has set and I must meet the others in the study for sherry after dinner."

Jonathan helped Victoria reassemble her clothes and pin up her hair.

"Your golden hair is wasted in this knot every day. Its beauty is my secret. My luscious treat."

"Jonathan you must not lose sight of the situation at hand. Button me!" Victoria insisted.

"My time with you was short but it was enchanting. Worthy of the risk."

"I will send word for you soon Victoria."

****

The Duke and Lady Hawthorne made the flat on Hingham their own. Jonathan made plans, each more clever than the last. They managed to steal away directly under Lord Hawthorne's nose. He was pleased that his wife was always so happy and did not question the reason.

It was turning into something neither expected – love.

Times were tumultuous in London that season. Every day there was a new set of visitors. Lady Hawthorne did her share of calling as well. It was her time with Jonathan that she valued most and she was too busy to care where their liaison might lead.

The Duke of Wellington was becoming emotionally torn up over the circumstance. He could not forget that Victoria was a married woman. There were titles, reputations and most of all hearts to consider. Jonathan was confused. He had to devise a plan.

CHAPTER TEN

The Duke was not in good spirits. He could determine from the silence that the day was young. He would use the moments he had to clear his head. Lord Hawthorne was in Kent for a few days and he needed to get a note to Victoria. They had managed to see each other daily and she was expecting to meet with him at perhaps the boathouse after dark. The Duke would see his Victoria and that had to be the last time. He would need help from Elizabeth, Oliver and the man who had been their courier. Jonathan composed a note for Victoria.

~~*Dearest Victoria*~~

The words would not come easy. It was not his desire to write this last note to the only woman he had ever loved.

Dearest Victoria:

The boathouse at sundown.

Your Jonathan

He could not write further. After breakfast, he would pass his final letter to the courier. He sealed it with blue wax, with no distinctive insignia. He placed it in his coat pocket.

"Good Morning Lady Elizabeth. You are pretty in pink today and your face glows. I would think you had a dalliance if I did not know better." Jonathan greeted his sister as he poured a cup of very black tea which he was having free of cream or any other support.

"Must it always be about some sort of bedroom antics that cause such affects? Tis Sunday and I am excited about the Persimmon House ball next weekend. I am just happy Duke, which does occasionally happen to a spinster like I." Elizabeth was tired of riding her brothers moods and she sensed today was a bad one.

"I need your assistance with a matter. Oliver! You can come in now, as your aid is needed as well. Will save me if I do not have to repeat my words." Oliver joined Lady Elizabeth and Jonathan.

"I will see Lady Hawthorne tonight. It shall be the last. Tonight is so that I may take one final look at the Lady before I move on."

"Tighten your reins Oliver. This is going to be an unpleasant and bumpy affair as expected." Elizabeth warned.

"I am aware Lady" Oliver responded.

"I am weary of the comments as they are unnecessary. I said from the start that this would have an end. It took more time than perhaps I should have allowed. She is a young girl, and married. I temporarily took leave of my senses."

"I will await instruction Sir" Oliver stiffened.

"I will tell the lady, at our meeting tonight that the following day will take me to town center the next day. She will also take to the gardens within London as she is to picnic with you Lady Elizabeth. You will set up the affair. The basket will be celebratory. Have the courier prepare it for you. Oliver says he can perform any task when asked. You will have Lady Hawthorne in high spirits. I will handle the rest."

"Do I send Lady Hawthorne a formal invitation for the picnic?" Elizabeth asked.

"Yes. I wish you to invite Lady Elaine also. The more associates present will spread evidence of my crudeness. Have Ladies Sophie and Hannah join the event as well. The gossip will spread. Lady Hawthorne will not speak out loud but the message will be as sharp as a saber."

"Brother, why do you not speak the truth to the lady tonight? It is more humane than said foolery." Elizabeth queried.

"I must have one final night with Victoria. I want one tryst with her before I return her to Lord Hawthorne."

"She is not property Sir Duke." Oliver stepped out of character.

"You are my servant. I have included you in such matters because I pay you plenty. You know of no matters of the heart. Lady Hawthorne is property of mine. I found her and I am returning her to the proper owner. Her husband."

"Jonathan I cannot know what has come over you. You are acting like a crude monster. To talk to Oliver with such harsh words is….."

Oliver interrupted. "Lady Elizabeth, The Duke of Wellington is correct to return me to my place as a hired man. Is there anything I can do to make your plan run smoothly?"

The Duke adjusted himself and cleared his throat. "I shall make the courier busy today. I need this note sent to Lady Hawthorne through the maid. I will also have a message to be sent to Lady Celeste from the end street in Wandsworth."

"Lady Celeste?" Elizabeth could only shake her head.

Lady Celeste was a woman many knew. She was equal to the Duke of Wellington in reputation if not title. She would be an excellent pawn. She would know she was being used as such but it was within her nature not to care. The Duke composed a note to Celeste.

> *Celeste*
>
> *It is my desire to walk through the common with you tomorrow. A carriage will be sent for you at 12 Noon. If it is not within your ability to join me, please send word.*

The Duke of Wellington

The note was signed, sealed and handed to the courier with the note to Lady Hawthorne. Jonathan suspended the remainder of the day. He would rest until his meeting with Victoria at sundown.

****

Esther handed the note to Lady Hawthorne. She opened it quickly, as she had been expecting correspondence. It was brief and written in a shaky hand. Jonathan was known to express himself with bold confidence in letters. She was only pleased that they should meet at the boathouse that evening. She was having breakfast with Ladies Hannah and Sophie. They provided company when Lord Hawthorne was away.

"Good morning Lady Hawthorne" Sophie was the first to welcome her in the dining room.

"It is a good morning. I do hope Lord Hawthorne is having his peace at Derby Manor."

"I am sure. James is in his company to assure all of his needs are met. He will have time to read his Bible. Father is most intelligent and dedicated to his Book." Hannah added.

Victoria wanted to say he was devoted to his Gin. That is all James would be providing Lord Hawthorne. She knew however that those were not words to share with his angelic daughters. She had grown to accept her husband for what he offered. She had Jonathan to think of and her rising rank in society. Victoria was happy with her world.

****

As the sun was setting Victoria prepared for Jonathan. They would meet at the place where they first made love on the hard surface of the table. Victoria had revisited the boathouse several times since to relive that perfect evening. She had arranged one of the bunks with proper linens and cushions that would go un-missing from the main house. If anyone were to come upon the arrangements, she would say it was a place for her to reflect.

She wore pink, which she knew Jonathan favored with several layers for her lover to remove. He delighted in the ritual. With perfume dabbed down her neck, she created a sensory path for Jonathan to follow. She fastened her hair with a single pin. When released it would provide the affect Jonathan desired.

With Lord Hawthorne away, she would not have to worry about him noticing her absence. If this were ever the case.

Victoria walked to the end of the dock, careful to avoid the rotted boards. The sky was star lit but there was only a sliver of a moon. Enough, Victoria thought. Jonathan stood at the doorway to the boathouse. The Duke of Wellington was enjoying the silence and cool of an early summer evening. It would be the final time he would approach his love with honest intentions. Henceforth, it would be a cruel rouse. One he was forced to undertake to save titles, land and reputations although hearts would be sacrificed.

"My beautiful lady. I would create a portrait of you as you stand amongst the stars but my skills could not do you justice. Hello Victoria."

"Jonathan, you have not been standing there long?"

"Never long enough. Come to me my darling. Into the place we began our liaison."

"Jonathan, you make our love sound temporary by the use of such words." Victoria bounced back.

With that, the Duke of Wellington carried Lady Hawthorne into the bunkroom, where they carried on until the sun rose.

"I must get back to the house. I will say I was out for a morning stroll. No one will be wise to our meeting."

"Victoria, you look different to me. Perhaps it is because I do not get to see you at this early hour. The lighting suits you. You are wearing the sapphire earrings. They match the sparkle in your eyes. Please always hold them near and think of me when you lay your blue eyes upon them."

"Jonathan I shall receive a note of our next meeting?"

"The house awaits you love. You must go now"

The blood left Jonathans face as Victoria ran out of the boathouse. She was light and smiling. She was happy, how he would remember her.

****

"Lady Hawthorne, I have your daily schedule of events. You are to have an outing today in the commons with Ladies Elizabeth, Hannah, Sophie and Elaine. The note came today from Lady Elizabeth and the weather is agreeable to view the gardens."

"Thank you for the alert Blanche. Do you know if Lord Hawthorne is to return from Derby Manor as scheduled?"

"If his schedule holds he will be back by sundown. You may catch up at dinnertime. That is all I have on your schedule for today Lady."

Victoria was curious if she had received word from Jonathan but perhaps it was slipped to his sister to deliver during their outing. She would dress in a light colored frock. Esther would join the ladies as chaperone and she would handle the parasol. It would be a grand time to share stories.

****

"Are not the roses more abundant than ever?" Hannah remarked.

"I would say you are correct sister. I will make sure I have many fresh cut by the gardener to wear with my dress at this weekend's ball. It shall be a grand affair."

"It will Lady Sophie. I will be escorted by my brother, The Duke of Wellington."

Victoria was only half listening to the other ladies. It seemed that Elizabeth had no note from Jonathan. She was distracted. She and Lady Elaine were enjoying some grapes and cheese

"Well, funny coincidence. There is the Duke as we speak."

Across the common, Jonathan was conversing with Lady Celeste. Victoria was familiar with The Duke's techniques. See could see him whispering to her and by her laughter, it was flirtation.

"The Duke is known for his conquests." Spoke Hannah.

"I have heard they number in the hundreds." Elaine joined in. "He leans in towards Lady Celeste. I dare say she will be his next.

"My brother has returned to being quite the bon vivant. Celeste does very well with men of title." Elizabeth looked to Victoria. She was frozen.

Esther rescued her lady. "I think we have spoken our tongues too much. You seem to have lost Color Lady Hawthorne. Perhaps the heat is too much. We should lead back to the carriage."

Victoria had forgotten to remove the sapphires from her ears that morning. She discretely ripped them from her lobes when she settled in the carriage.

CHAPTER ELEVEN

Victoria and Esther rode most of the way back to Nansen Court in silence. Victoria shouted to the chauffeur.

"Hingham Road. I want the carriage to go to Hingham Road immediately."

The carriage changed direction. Esther was confused. Victoria released the floodgate. Her face was rouged and her cheeks wet. The earrings she clenched in her fists drew blood from her palms. The carriage careened through the London streets.

"This is madness Lady. Where do we travel? I warned you the Duke of Wellington was nothing but a scoundrel. He is not deserving of your desperation. Sweet God pray for us!" Esther shouted above the cacophonous roar of the galloping horses and the brutal sound of the whip.

"FASTER." Victoria cried.

"Lady, please speak with."

"Number four Hingham Road." The carriage came to halt in front of the place that had been so magical to her and Jonathan. She did not know what she would find there. She knew not why she had taken the detour.

"Esther, you will please wait for me. I must take a look inside for it is where I left my heart."

Victoria dashed through the black iron gate. The door was ajar. She entered. The flat she had come to know that was kept so neat and smelled of lilies and manliness was a mess. It smelled of cloying jasmine, cheap musk and sour wine. There was a frock coat and a gaudy parasol discarded on the floor. The embers in the fireplace were still warm.

"Duke of Wellington! Show thine face you appalling creature. I can smell you and that harlot. Come show your face coward." Lady Hawthorne screamed as she raced through the bedrooms. One showed that its recent visitors had used the bed. Linens were askew and pillows lay on the floor. There was no person in the flat. Victoria was leaving when she came across a piece of crimson silk fabric attached with a single pearl. Victoria released upon it two simple bloodied sapphires.

Victoria climbed back into the carriage to a frightened Esther. She directed the chauffer to return to Sherborne slowly.

"Esther, you advised me of the Duke. I did not heed your warnings. I was a silly girl who surrendered myself to the man – fully. I have risked all for Jonathan and I dared think he loved me. I am not to recover from this tragedy. How do I approach my husband after this?"

"My sweet Victoria. Your heart is tender but it is mendable. Time will pass to revel this as an error. It pains me to see you so pained." Esther held her Lady in her ample lap.

"I must put on an act for Lord Hawthorne. He is to return to Sherborne at sundown. I certainly cannot explain my disposition. You must say I am depleted due to the rigors of the outing. I need your absolute silence in this matter. It is a past that no one will ever hear of."

"You have my honor as always Victoria. Word will not come from my lips. I should think Lady Elizabeth will respect your wishes and Jonathan gains nothing from spreading the news. You go quickly to your bed and I will delicately explain your absence to Lord Hawthorne.

****

The Duke of Wellington was terse to Lady Celeste when the carriage pulled through Wandsworth. Victoria had seen him and surely, she saw the flat, which he had staged to further his plan. The openings of the carriage were covered to protect his privacy as it was beyond good taste to ride with a woman alone. He had taken such a ride before and onlookers knew the truth behind the shroud. London would be talking of his return to his old ways. Victoria would be privy to all. Her tender heart would be repeatedly broken.

"You walked with me through the common. It was my desire. I am finished with you now and you may take leave." Jonathan stated.

"Duke. We may further the affair within the confines and privacy of my home. It is not as lavish as your own but it should provide." Celeste purred.

"You may go Lady"

With a frown, Celeste disappeared into her modest home. Jonathan returned to his house in London. He had hoped to disappear to his room but waiting in the drawing room were his sister and Oliver.

"I was at the common with the ladies today. We were enjoying the day. Victoria viewed your indiscretion as planned. She was struck by silence Jonathan. With a brutal blow, you shattered the girl. You have taken so much from her that I doubt she will recover. I feel dirty that I have aided in your cruelty and I will no longer play in this game of treachery." Elizabeth scolded and Oliver stood in silence.

"What would you have me do? I indeed stole her one precious gift. I robbed the fair lady of her purity of both body and soul. It had to be swift and fierce. There was no allowance for love and she realizes now I am unworthy of such strong emotion. Oliver, I have behaved badly to you, as I treated you as a paid man. Know that I value your friendship and loyalty. My disposition is bad so I will spend days by myself. I will return to Hingham Road where I wish to remain unbothered until I emerge renewed. Oliver, have the courier pack my trunk and provide supplies in the flat so I have sustenance in my exile."

The Duke exited the drawing room. Lady Elizabeth reached out to her brother and Oliver held her back.

"Let the Duke alone Lady." Oliver spoke with sympathy through his glance. Elizabeth understood.

****

Victoria lay beneath her blankets. She left Esther to explain to Mavis and the ladies the reason for her absence. Victoria felt ill. She had been through a great deal in her emotion. It occurred to her that it should be time for her monthly discomfort. The two combined would surely cause the distress she was feeling. Victoria went back to sleep under her layers of puffs.

She dreamed of her times spent at Hingham Road. For the first time in her life, she felt at ease. She would forget to have her hair combed and with her feet elevated on the table, she read the poems of Eleanor Barrett and Robert Browning. She would sometimes read aloud to Jonathan and he would listen closely to every word. They would be affected by the words on the page and fall into each other. They had a natural rhythm while making love. It could not be denied.

Jonathan knew parts of her body well. Places below that she did not know existed. He taught her and he learned from her. It was as if they were one. Victoria enjoyed herself with no lack of confidence. She was not embarrassed of her naked body. Jonathan taught her love and appreciation for herself. No one had dared try before.

Victoria recalled the words of Lord Byron.

> *She walks in beauty, like the night*
>
> *Of cloudless climes and starry skies;*
>
> *And all that's best of dark and bright*
>
> *Meet in her aspect and her eyes:*
>
> *Thus mellowed to that tender light*
>
> *Which heaven to gaudy day denies*

She could clearly hear them as Jonathan whispered into her ears. He may as well have penned them himself. She physically desired for just a moment of the bliss she felt while in her lover's arms.

****

It had been two days and Victoria had not begun her monthly as anticipated. She had thought her exhaustion was a result of her regular schedule but she still showed no sign of bleeding. The Countess was not be one to confide in. She was not the one to warn her of her monthly disability. She would discuss the fear she had, that perhaps she may be with child, with Esther.

"Hello love." Esther poked her head into Victoria's room. Her maid had been cautious to leave her to recover. There were no new notes to send and the others in the household, including Lord Hawthorne seemed satisfied with her explanations. It was not uncommon for the Lady to take down for a week when she was convalescing. The calendar told her story.

"Please come in Esther. Rest has not provided me with relief in my heart nor my body. I am worried Esther, that my love has come with a price. I fear I am with child. If this is the case it must be as a result of my relations with the Duke of Wellington." Victoria spoke clearly. She was frightened out of her reveries.

"I see a change in you my dear. If you are but one day out of your schedule." Esther stopped.

"I know my body Esther. I have terrible food cravings. My size seven feet are continually more difficult to fit my size six boots."

Esther empathized. "Lord Hawthorne must know Victoria. This is not a secret you can hold back from the man. It will be apparent as time moves forward."

"Esther have there been no notes from the courier?"

"No Lady Hawthorne."

"Please leave me alone Esther so I can consider my future." Victoria showed tears.

"I will be within a voice call from your side Victoria. You shall have time. You must proceed with sensitivity to your title and place in society. Lord Hawthorne is a kind man. He is a father to you and a proud gentleman who you must consider."

"I hear you Esther. I will keep in mind your words of wisdom. I would not be in such trouble if I had done so before."

****

Victoria was out of bed and with Esther's aid she dressed in a powder blue dress with wide blue sleeves and lace tiered down the skirt. She was looking refreshed and ready to face her husband. She had cleared her schedule with the help of Mavis. It was time to reveal her condition. The ball at Persimmon House was the following evening. She would attend. Her dear Aunt, the Lady Rose Sterling, hosted it. It would be necessary to make an appearance on the arm of her husband to quiet any rumors surrounding her absence. She would begin the day at breakfast with Lord Hawthorne and his daughters.

"Good morning Thomas." Victoria kissed her husband on the cheek. She said her hellos to Sophie and Hannah.

"You look better Lady. I have left you alone at Esther's advisement. Your condition seems to be resolved. Your complexion is the color of a ripe peach. I have missed you my wife."

"I am back as you see. Would you delight me with a stroll through the rose garden after our meal?"

"I will be honored. I promise not to speak of my Bible if you hold your tongue about winged creatures."

"I agree Lord Hawthorne. I shall be present on the front steps waiting for you. I prefer we have our privacy." Victoria added.

"Do tell us you are well enough to attend the ball." Sophie spoke up.

"Yes Sophie. I plan to attend the ball with Lord Hawthorne as my escort of course." Victoria responded.

"It should be a grand event. I expect to see Lady Elizabeth with her brother. It will be a show to see him after his public inappropriateness." Hannah interjected.

"He is a scalawag. He is undeserving of his title."

"I agree Sophie; he is Duke of the bedroom." Hannah delighted in the banter.

Victoria ignored the nonsense. She could not show an interest, as it might reveal her connection to the Duke.

"Daughters, we must not speak poorly of one we have entertained in our home. I have had much time to devote to scripture and this talk is not within my ideals."

"We are sorry if we have spoken out of line."

"Thank you Hannah. We must live by the Good Book. Am I correct Lady?"

"Yes Lord." Victoria agreed.

****

Lord and Lady Hawthorne began their stroll through the roses and by the fountains on the property at Nansen Court. They joined arms and spoke of the differing colors abounding in the blooms. There was no fog or mist about which was rare for an early afternoon in London. Victoria was timid but resolute as she let Thomas into the truth about her infidelity and present condition.

"Dear husband. I must reveal the truth to you through my words. I promised to protect your name and I have failed. I have found my way into the arms of another."

Lord Hawthorne was without words. He had not expected this to come out of Victoria's mouth. He recalled the words she said to him.

"I promise to honor you Lord Hawthorne, my husband."

Victoria continued. "It was short lived and now it has ended. We were very cautious. Your name will not be involved in scandal. I made an error that will change the rest of our lives Thomas. I am so shamed. I seek your forgiveness, as it is all I have. I give you my honesty and fidelity from this moment forth."

"You have lied to me Lady. You have made a mockery of our marital contract." Lord Hawthorne sat down on a nearby bench. The walk and the unexpected news had made him short of breath.

"That is not all. I am with the man's child."

"Lady Hawthorne, you must repeat those words." Thomas was stunned

"My scheduled expectations did not come this month. I am sure of it. I am with a child Sir."

"Do you know he is the responsible party?"

"Yes. He has been the only one but as I said it is over. It was only a dalliance which I deeply regret."

"I will retire to the library Victoria. I have a lot to consider. You may find me there in an hour's time. Discretion is of paramount importance. Be prepared to tell me all involved in this sordid affair for there must have been accomplices to your duplicitous scheme."

Victoria returned to her room before rejoining Thomas in the library. She was afraid of naming Esther, for fear he might release her. She would have no hopes of employment beyond Sherborne and she was the only support Victoria had remaining. She could not mention Lady Elizabeth or Oliver, as they would lead back to the Duke of Wellington. She had caused pain through her lies and now her silence would be required to protect those she loved. Victoria would be asked the name of her lover and she would not release it. She inhaled deeply and went to the library.

"Have you had significant time to consider the matter my Lord?"

"Victoria, please enter."

"You have humiliated me. You have destroyed the dignity of an old man who is responsible for your rank in society and the very floors you walk upon. Your father, the Earl and I entered into this contract based on your high morals. We trusted you.

You were also expected to provide an heir. A son to carry on my good name and reputation. I admit my negligence in the bedroom but it does not provide you with an excuse. I love you too much my dear, to drag your name through scum. We will go to the country at Derby Manor where you will deliver our child. It will be expertly handled and not spoken of when we leave these four walls."

Victoria fell to her knees and begged her husband's forgiveness.

"I do not deserve you Sir. You must let me prove myself as the woman you married. I will deliver the child unto you as your son. If it is not a boy, we will work to produce one until it happens. I will do anything for you Thomas."

"Get off your knees Victoria. I only ask his name,"

"I cannot deliver what you ask."

"I will find the name without your assistance Victoria. I am cleverer than you are. I will see you at mealtime. We go to Persimmon House tomorrow for the ball and then we will retreat to the country. Go back to your room and rinse your face."

CHAPTER TWELVE

The Duke of Wellington arrived home from Hingham Road. He had spent a few days ruminating the recent events with Victoria. He was ashamed of what she was thinking of him. His trickery ran deep. He knew this as he cleaned up the mess he had created to make it look as if he had a tryst with Lady Celeste. He knew she would smell the Jasmine, which she detested and the musk, which she did not fancy. He had worn it the night they danced at the Marshall's home in Chelsea. She later commented that she loved his natural scent and he no longer bothered with cologne.

He left behind his calling card, the red silk, so she would think he had a habit of giving it to all of the ladies. She did not realize that the red fabric with a pearl was the last remembrance he had of his father. He only shared it with Victoria. The Duke was not thin-skinned but he sobbed when he found the bloodied sapphires. He longed to kiss any part of her body that had incurred harm.

Jonathan realized he must present a jovial front at Persimmon House. Lord and Lady Hawthorne would attend. He needed to hold his composure. He could not dare ask for

Victoria's hand in a dance. The risk of discovery was too great.

"Are you still planning to join me at the ball this evening Lady Elizabeth" The Duke found Elizabeth in the drawing room working on needlework. Oliver was nearby.

"I am brother. It is good to have you home where you belong. Hingham Road is no place for a man accustomed to a convivial lifestyle, although it is charming."

"You have not been to the flat on Hingham Road Elizabeth. Have you?"

"As I said Duke, welcome home. You bring levity to the house. Are you prepared to see Victoria? If I may inquire." Elizabeth continued, ignoring his question.

"I have had time to think about Lady Hawthorne and her husband. I will have no difficulties seeing the married couple at the ball. I will have a full set of young ladies to occupy me with dance."

"I am certain Jonathan. I have heard word that the Baron is looking for a suitable mate for his daughter Madeline. He is very particular in choosing a mate for his daughters. They closely resemble his wife who died tragically, may she rest in peace. It is about time for you to find a wife dear brother."

"You have heard word of many things Elizabeth. You ladies talk too much. If Lady Madeline has an opening for my dance, I will make a proposal." Jonathan had a laugh, which he frequently had with his sister.

"May I assist you with your attire Sir?"

"Music to my ears Oliver. You have been quiet since my arrival home my friend. What has happened to the man who raised me since I was 10 years old?"

"I am you're hired butler Sir Duke. I am presenting the respect you pay me for each month."

"I must keep proving my love for you as a member of this small family. It will be my quest. My apology seems to have been ignored. I was considering having that cousin of yours hired on. Would he be amenable to such an offer?"

"The cousin who served as your courier has moved on to apprentice as a butler at a manor in the country. He is not giving of details. It is said to be a grand arrangement. We, or rather I, will miss his presence nearby."

"Does this courier/cousin have a moniker?"

"He is James."

"My father's name. I shall make sure I find where James lands. He has my highest recommendation."

****

"Esther this shall be my final ball before I go to the country with Lord Hawthorne. For a long time hence, I shall have swollen belly. Let us make the most of my form while it still exists. I want to create a dramatic affect. I wish to make my husband proud." Victoria insisted.

"I am pleased to see a smile upon your face. I have laid out your drawers and slip from your trousseau and we will follow with the corset."

"You must pull me in tight Esther. I have gone without today. They say I am to eat freely but I thought I would do no harm this once."

"I have two petticoats, a camisole and your bustle prepared. Finally, I have your lilac dress of satin. It has been imported from Paris. I dare say it is your most grand."

Victoria remembered any shade of purple was Jonathan's favorite. He liked it as a compliment to her ivory skin and blue eyes. She would see The Duke at the ball. She knew not how she would react.

"Come out of your daydream Lady. It is to be a festive occasion and thinking of the Duke will bring a pallor over the event."

Victoria looked elegant in her gown. It was off the shoulder with short-capped sleeves. Her back and neck were bare. She garnished with an emerald necklace that matched her wedding ring. The back was pleated five ways leading to a small satin train. Decoration was delicately embroidered lace and pearls.

"I am not comfortable Esther. My breath is restricted."

"Perfect." Esther joked.

****

Lord and Lady Hawthorne entered Persimmon House. They dropped their apparel at the cloakroom and were led into the ballroom. Those greeting them were many. Lady Sterling took Victoria's hand first. She was followed by a line consisting of familiar faces, Earl and Countess Tompkins, Peter and the honorable Jane Marley, Lady Elaine, Lady Sara and Lady Diana who had recently given birth.

"It is lovely to see you both. Welcome to Persimmon House. The staff is here to serve you."

"Lady Sterling you must include me on your card so I may share a dance with you." Lord Hawthorne gave a proper bow.

Victoria noticed Baron Stephan with Madeline and Hannah across the room. They approached the familiar friends. They chatted with them about their plans for the autumn months ahead and many mannered subjects.

"This is meant to be our final occasion this season. We are packing for Kent where we will spend quiet months at Derby Manor. I have not had the occasion to spend time at the Manor. You will have to pay us a visit." Lady Hawthorne stopped speaking.

"Lord and Lady Hawthorne, Baron, ladies. I know I have not made the acquaintance of Ladies Madeline and Hannah. Allow me to introduce myself. I am Jonathan Duke of Wellington."

His green eyes glowed and while he spoke, his hand met Victoria. It was momentary but it caused a flood of memories to return. Jonathan knew the strength of his touch. He was also moved to remember his time alone with Victoria. Elizabeth was by his side and she nudged Jonathan to remind him where he stood.

"I wish that Lady Madeline might join me for a dance." The Duke finally spoke but it was not to Victoria. She was devastated but not surprised. He would never take the risk.

"Yes Duke. It would be my pleasure to dance with you."

Madeline and Jonathan took to the dance floor, they held each other appropriately and there were no words spoken. It was not as the dance Victoria shared with the Duke in Chelsea.

"My Lord. I am feeling warm would you escort me to the door so that I may take a short stroll in the gardens."

"Why of course I will escort you. Would you like me to join you outdoors?"

"I will be fine alone. I need only catch my breath."

"I will wait for your return."

Victoria could not take her eyes off the Duke. It caused pain to see him dance with Lady Madeline. A spell outside would save her from despair. She stopped by a light pink rose. She favored them above all others.

"The flower does not compare to your beauty Victoria"

"Jonathan! What of Lady Madeline."

"The dance completed and my eyes and heart followed you here. I was a fool in the commons with Lady Celeste. I tried to cause you pain. I can tell by the creases below your sky blue eyes that you have cried. I caused you pain?"

"Like no other. The death of my dear Mary changed me, but my pain at your hands stopped me."

"I leave for the country soon. I am to be there with my husband."

"You are his. I let you go."

"You stole from me and now I must forever live with the shame."

"My sweet Victoria. One final kiss is all I ask. I will free you to be the married lady you were born to be."

"No Jonathan. I cannot consent."

Jonathan wrapped Victoria in tight embrace. His breathe and scent rendered her helpless. He kissed her long and purposeful on her lips.

Victoria ran back to the ballroom, passing Lord Hawthorne who was in the doorway. He glared at his wife and moved her aside while he rushed towards the Duke. Victoria was sure her husband would fall but he weighed heavily on his black cane. He shook his stick at the Duke.

"You sir have no place near my wife. You are never to contact my Lady. Not lay an eye upon her. She is my property. You have caused enough damage to my delicate Victoria. You know this – I am a smarter man than you. I have power over you. Be very careful man." Lord Hawthorne spat on Jonathan's shoes. He returned to his wife. Lord and Lady Hawthorne made excuses and returned to Sherborne. The Duke of Wellington wiped off his toes with a leaf. He was perplexed by Lord Hawthorne's words of caution.

CHAPTER THIRTEEN

The ride home from Persimmon house was tense. Recent events had instilled a new confidence in Victoria. There was nothing left to hide from Lord Hawthorne. She was free to speak freely.

"I am sorry Thomas. It was a goodbye kiss. You must believe that it was contrary to my wishes. He gave me no choice really." Victoria pleaded.

"I believe you woman. I found out the name prior to your indiscretion at the ball. I do not fear that this will happen again. The man has no power over me. My hope is that he does not know you are with child."

"No, My Lord. The Duke has no reason to think that he is to be a father."

"Those words just spoken are the reason we are spending months in the country. The Duke of Wellington is not the FATHER. I am to be the child's father. You will never refer to the Duke as such again. I have a plan for everything. Hence forth you will forget the man exists."

"Yes my Lord."

Once back at Nansen Court Lady Victoria returned to her solitary room. Boxes and trunks were on display everywhere. The packing had begun. Her trousseau had barely been touched. Many of her things would be packed away until after she had the child. She would be growing fat and there was no use for them. Victoria was sitting with the Countess and the Earl tomorrow. She would enjoy some time with her parents. She could use company. She was feeling very much alone. Her entrance into society had been positive for all to see but it had been an enormous failure to Victoria. Esther helped her undress. She noticed the door adjoining her quarters with those of her husband was ajar. There was a new sense about, that did not sit well with Lady Hawthorne. She was constantly under watch. In slumber, her favorite moments, there would be eyes upon her. Privacy was gone.

"Good Morning Lady Sophie. Lady Hannah it is nice to see you this morning. Lord Hawthorne." Victoria kissed her husband and took her chair at the dining room table.

"Hello Lady. I trust you slept well last night. I laid my eyes upon your resting form on a couple of occasions to assure you were resting well." Lord Hawthorne commented.

"My dear husband. You need not check on me while I sleep."

"I am merely keeping an eye open for what is mine." Thomas winked. He was proud of himself.

The ladies laughed. They did not know the meaning hiding beneath Lord Hawthorne's comment. He was acting as though he caught the largest fox on a hunt. The message was clear to his wife. She was but a prize and her husband had indeed won.

"I was surprised by your sudden departure from the Ball last night father."

"I am sorry you were troubled Sophie. Lady Hawthorne was still getting over her recent weakness and she could no longer tolerate the excitement at Persimmon House. We will be taking the journey to the country in a number of days. Rest was needed."

"I danced every set. I had the pleasure of two dances with John Tully. We played together as children. I remember him to have an offensive odor."

"And now sister does his aroma repel you." Sophie questioned.

"I should say the honorable Mr. Tully is most agreeable. He is going to enter his military service in September. He will wear the uniform of the Royal Navy. Father, I think he may ask permission to correspond with me while he is away. I am open to such if you are agreeable." Hannah was giving her father notice.

"My dear Hannah. You will have many suitors at social season next. I do not think a letter will be of any harm. I will wait for John Tully's visit. Please keep in mind he carries no title and his family is not landed. That will be foremost in my mind when picking a suitable mate for my daughter." Lord Hawthorne advised.

"The Duke of Wellington had three dances with Lady Madeline. They seem to be a good match if Baron Stephan can forgive the Duke of his reputation."

Victoria bristled inside at the mention of the Duke's name. She could show no reaction as Lord Hawthorne was carefully watching. To further test his wife, the Lord commented.

"Well, Sophie thank you for such gossip. I think that would be a fine match. Do you agree Lady?"

"Befitting. Yes, I suppose so. I cannot say I know either party beyond social calling." Victoria managed to get out a comment.

"Not so my Lady. You have spent days at Markham with Lady Madeline and Lady Elizabeth is a close confident so you must have some knowledge of her brother." Lord Hawthorne was having a grand time watching his wife's discomfort.

"As I have said Lord. The match is befitting." A short sentence was all Victoria could manage.

Victoria was being punished for her infidelity. Any mention of the Duke made her insides tumble. It was intensified due to her current state. Perhaps life at the Manor would make Lord Hawthorne think less about the Duke.

"We will be receiving the Earl and Countess today. They desire to wish us well before our departure. I can expect to see you in the Parlor Victoria?"

"Yes of course, but they are my parents and you are not required to be present. You are free to prepare your papers to bring to the Manor."

"Lady Hawthorne. I plan to by your side always during this period of transition. I have a new young man working with James and a new lady to be with you."

"What of Esther? That is not a subject I will negotiate."

Lord Hawthorne dealt with the subject delicately as he was aware Sophie and Hannah were present. He was becoming adept at using other's as witness to his words with Victoria. She was not likely to protest when an audience was present.

"I would never remove Esther from your side. She has been with you for many years and I realize she is your closest confidant. I am aware of her advancing age and thought she would benefit from an extra pair of hands. Liza is the young girl I have chosen. She will be like a shadow to dear old Esther. It is not my practice to put honored long time servants out. I only gently shepherd them into retirement. There are spacious out buildings at Derby Manor where dear Esther can remain close by."

"Look Lady Hawthorne. Father is caring for you and those close to you. We are so lucky to have such a devoted man looking out for us." Sophie heaped praise upon her father.

Victoria returned to her room before she received The Earl and Countess. She knew her husband was working to remove her freedom. His plan was carefully created and she could not remember a time when she had been so isolated. She had the feeling of complete freedom while in Jonathan's arms. She did as Mary told her. She learned to laugh. She was a slave now. Her most trusted friend, Esther was being made irrelevant.

She was fumbling through one of her trunks which had been packed by Liza and new members of the staff, who were appearing to help pack up the house. It contained her memories. Most of the costumes were ones that had been carefully removed by the Duke. With every layer he laid to the floor, Victoria became closer to freedom. She was able to shed the constrictions of being Lady

Hawthorne. She searched through folds of tulle and her brightest pinks and lilacs.

"Hello my Lady. You have come upon the trunk I have been searching for."

"Yes Liza. These are among my favorite things."

"The ladies travelling on the liner to America will appreciate your thoughtful donation. They are mostly of Irish decent and have little more than the clothes on their back. Lord Hawthorne said this trunk is only a portion of your generous donation. You are a lucky lady to have a tailor waiting for you at Derby Manor to sew you a new wardrobe. Lord Hawthorne had his close secretary Martha choose the fabrics to be imported from Paris and Milan. The colors will suit you."

"Liza, there must be some error in your instruction. These clothes will be suitable for next season. They will have to be altered to keep step with fashion but otherwise they are fine."

Liza closed the trunk of memories shut, nearly injuring Victoria's hand. Victoria began to shudder. Esther was nowhere in sight. This is how it would be. Her husband wanted no reminders of the Duke. It was her punishment and it was having the desired effect.

"I know it is difficult to let something go that is so beautiful. You are going to be fitted with colors and styles more appropriate for a married lady."

Lady Hawthorne had no choice but to allow the torture to continue. Like waves in the ocean, it rolled over her. She was as a sturdy jagged cliff. Lord Hawthorne had planned she become a bland ocean stone. Pretty to look at and danger to no one.

****

Before she went downstairs to meet with her parents, Victoria checked to see if her condition was showing yet. She was still thin and light. She and Lord Hawthorne would not announce the expectance of their child until she had time to settle in at Derby Manor. Her largest hurdle would be explaining her absence at her brother's wedding celebration to Jane. Lord Hawthorne probably had a plan in place. He had thought of everything. It was necessary to keep her condition secret, as to not alert the Duke. He need only do the simple calculations to discover the child was his own. Victoria proceeded to the parlor.

****

"Thomas you have arrived early. Do you not trust me to be alone with my own parents?"

"Time my dear Victoria. You do not earn trust so easily. I was careless to leave you to your own whims. It is not a mistake I intend to make again. This phase will pass. I am only showing my love for you Victoria. Restrictions may be harsh but they are necessary."

"Lord Hawthorne, can I expect no privacy henceforth? I am aware of my generous donations. They are only belongings and I will heal."

"You feign a lack of caring my dear. I know the things that hold as reminders of your infidelity with the Duke of Wellington. They are not to be under my roof. We start anew at Derby Manor. Your Duke will cease to be a memory. I am making it simple for you to forget." Lord Hawthorne smiled.

"As you wish my Lord" Victoria smiled back.

James escorted the Earl and Countess to the couch. Mavis served them tea of hibiscus flower and butter crackers.

"We are aware you are leaving Sherborne for the country. Is rather hasty an exit?" The Earl spoke first.

"We are anxious to begin life as a family away from the restrictions applied by a full society schedule." Lord Hawthorne answered appropriately.

"How are you doing mother? It has been a hectic season for you with Mary's death, the Ball and now Peter's nuptials."

"I am busy but it takes away from my sadness, I have many blessings to count Victoria. I am proud that you wear the title of Lady Hawthorne so well. I can only imagine the time will soon arrive that you begin a family of your own."

"Marie! We spoke of not prying into personal matters between our daughter and her husband." The Earl tersely commented.

"As husband of the Lady, I can assure you that God willing; we will have news of a child soon. Getting away from the pressures in London is part of the plan. The distractions here are many." Lord Hawthorne had all the answers.

The Countess spoke. "Was a pleasant event at Persimmon House was it not?"

Victoria could not think of the ball without reliving the kiss. The Duke was handsome in his dark tails and white tie. His face always glowed as if he had just run a mile, not as Lord Hawthorne had glowed after too much gin.

"Oh yes mother it was grand."

"Lady Hawthorne and I had the time to converse with Baron Stephan and his daughters. Madeline is nearly as fair as his dearly departed wife." Lord Hawthorne was aware of the sensitive nerves to touch.

"Lady Madeline is very much in resemblance to her mother, may she rest in peace. I viewed her dancing with the Duke of Wellington. What do you think of that match my Lady?" The Countess queried.

"I would think it befitting. I do not know why it is such a concern of those under this roof." Victoria quickly answered.

"My dear Victoria. We all enjoy seeing a good love match," Lord Hawthorne enjoyed seeing his wife squirm.

After an hour of questions and answers, the Earl and Countess departed. Victoria was exhausted. She left to rest for the following day's journey. The house had been packed away and all of the necessary trunks sent ahead to the country or donated.

****

Thomas waited in his study for expected visitors. A knock at the door revealed James and his apprentice James. Cloaked in disguise was another man, Oliver.

"Welcome to Sherborne Oliver and James. You are here at my invitation through my trusted butler James. I am to make you an offer that you will indeed accept. It will make you wealthy servants. I can provide you with more than the Duke of Wellington can and I will help you protect the ones you consider family. For as I know they *are* family"

Oliver and James had closely kept their secret from the Duke, that they were father and son. Only one other person knew that Lady Elizabeth was the mother. Elizabeth and Oliver fell in love while they were at the family chalet in Switzerland. They were able to keep their love a secret from Jonathan and hid away in Switzerland while Lady Elizabeth gave birth to young James. The boy lived in the shadows knowing home to be on Hingham Road. Elizabeth and Oliver were able to keep their love and their son a secret. James became accustomed to living a secret and came to be the very loyal aid to Oliver. He was the perfect sort to aid The Duke and Victoria carry on their affair.

Lord Hawthorne had done some probing and found James to be the courier. He easily pieced together the rest. He had come up with a way of using them in his plot to keep the tryst between the Duke and his Lady a secret. They would help him claim the unborn child for his own and keep the Duke of Wellington as a memory of Victoria's.

"I will have you apprentice under my butler James at Derby Manor James. To be my trusted manservant will afford you working for one of the most respected men in all of

England. You will be loyal to me only. No word about my wife will leave the walls of my manor." Lord Hawthorne continued.

"You Oliver are to remain with the Duke. You will apprise me of his movements and make certain that he is not occupied by my wife. He will inquire. Of that, there is no doubt but he will learn nothing. I would think he would be nicely occupied by Lady Madeline. She fell into this plan accidentally but I should think it is good fortune. You should encourage his courtship to Lady Madeline." Lord Hawthorne had finished his comments and he was prepared for questions.

"Lord Hawthorne, Lady Elizabeth and I have managed to keep our love and word of our son private. We have not intentionally harmed you. I am sorry that your marriage to Lady Hawthorne has suffered. I am committed to The Duke as a father to a son. Duplicity is not within my nature." Oliver was seeking a way out.

"Oliver, I encourage you to reconsider. Under James' tutelage, young James will blossom as a fine butler. He may even be the first in your family to escape the life of servitude. I will leave nothing unsaid." Lord Hawthorne cleared his throat. "If you do not consent to my arrangement I am afraid word will spread That Lady Elizabeth is a whore who gave birth to a bastard child born of a roll in the stables with a hired man. This all occurred under the very nose of the Duke of Wellington. I will bring down the Duke and your dear Elizabeth will be shamed."

"Father you must protect my mother and our dear Duke."

Glances were exchanged. Oliver and James stood as broken men, James could not help but feel pity and Lord Hawthorne smiled.

"Lord Hawthorne, Elizabeth is a smart lady. She will uncover your scheme." Oliver tried to reason.

"You seem to have a way with the lady. Make certain she does not."

"I will try sir. I do have one demand."

"You are in no position to demand Oliver." Lord Hawthorne shot back.

"I demand you apologize. Lady Elizabeth is no whore. Furthermore, Sir, you must expose James to literature and culture. If he is to escape the servitude to men like you he stands no chance without such things."

"I know such love. I had it once with the first Lady Hawthorne. In her honor, I apologize."

The meeting was over.

****

Lord and Lady Hawthorne arrived at Derby Manor. It was a massive stone structure, larger than the house at Markham. It was surrounded by acres of wild grasslands and a dairy farm. It appeared Gothic in style and intimidating at first glance. There were housing structures to accommodate the servants. They were large enough to dwarf Sherborne and they gave hint that there was an ample amount of hired help.

It was not a house, nor a mansion, but more akin to a castle. Victoria imagined the number of rooms inside. She was scared and convinced that the hallways were full of ghosts. She entered with Lord Hawthorne, James and James. James was new to Lady Hawthorne and he seemed like an odd choice for an apprentice. He was gawky and he carried himself like something he was not.

"It is grand and large my Lady but it is yours and you will grow accustomed to the opulence. You will settle into your quarters, which have been prepared for your taste. A door connects my room. Should you need me it is to remain unlocked."

"Of course it is Thomas. Is Esther's room nearby?"

"Liza will be here in the main house. Your Esther will be housed on the property. You will see her each day. She will enjoy reduced duty I am sure."

Lady Hawthorne bristled.

"We will have supper at eight. There will be a woman to escort you to the small dining hall. It will be the two of us only. Sophie and Hannah will join us in a couple of days' time. Please tell me dear Lady, if you are experiencing discomfort due to your condition."

"I am feeling well and I will see you at dinner this evening."

****

Victoria missed London terribly. She felt alone. The Duke was no longer a short carriage ride away and their flat on Hingham was left empty. She had a new life to begin as Lady of the Manor. Tomorrow she would receive new clothes for her new life. Her lily of the valley perfume was gone and replaced by some violet concoction favored by Lord Hawthorne. She would spend the next six months trying to create a new life before she becomes a mother. Victoria sobbed.

CHAPTER FOURTEEN

Victoria was only months away from giving birth to her child. She was spending most days in bed to avoid exertion. Lord Hawthorne insisted upon keeping his wife out of view. She was a reminder of the heartache caused by her infidelity. She had grown accustomed to spending a great deal of her time alone. Esther would be allowed to visit every day but Liza was always present. They were not able to share secrets. Feelings were bottled up inside in addition to her condition it made her feel restricted and very large.

"Hello Lady. I am here to see that all of your needs are met." Esther had made a visit to the main house. Liza was clever to pretend being occupied.

"I am glad to see you Esther. I would like my hair washed today. Can you perform it the way you always did when I was a girl?" Victoria asked.

"I would love to wash your golden hair my love. It is your crowning glory. May I wash Lady Hawthorne's hair Liza?"

"I do not see any harm in the matter." Liza agreed. "I can go to the garden and get some fresh Rosemary and mint leaves if you would like."

"Yes Liza that sounds perfect. It is just what I need to improve my spirits," Victoria agreed. She would have a chance to be with Esther alone.

"Esther we only have a few moments of privacy. You brush my hair to prepare it to be washed and I will talk. First I must know if you are well in retirement."

"It is the way it has been set forth. Lord Hawthorne make certain that all my needs are met."

"Jonathan would brush my hair at the flat in Hingham. It has been many months since I have uttered his name. Thomas thinks I have forgotten him. I miss him more than ever. I feel life moving within me. I still hold on to a piece of him. That is something that Lord Hawthorne cannot take from me. Esther it is servitude I am under. I am made to look like an old spinster with drab colors and high necks. It is fashionable but I favor pastels and a show of flesh. It is the way Jonathan will remember me." Victoria was speaking rapidly.

"I hear you my Lady. I would listen to you go on forever but we must consider who may be listening."

"Hello Esther." Lord Hawthorne appeared from his chambers. "I thought I heard voices. I thought you were to be at rest my darling."

"I have had rest Thomas. Is not a moment to visit allowed?"

"I care that you are well my love. Your state is fragile. I have grown accustomed to keeping my door ajar so I may hear you if you fall into distress. Where is your girl Liza?"

"Liza went to fetch some herbs and flowers to wash my hair. She will return any moment."

"You have beautiful hair Victoria. I like it best parted in the center and pulled back in a low closely nestled bun. You wear it too loose and do not often cover with a bonnet. I prefer it covered so that is my secret to enjoy; you try to appear too young my dear. I need not worry because it is said to grow course and unruly after you give birth. If the birth is strenuous, it may fall out. It would be a shame. You ladies enjoy your hair washing folly"

Lord Hawthorne had heard every word they spoke. He was subtle in letting them know that they were always observed. Victoria sighed. Liza returned and she observed while Esther washed her hair.

****

A room next to Lord Hawthorne was set up for a physician. It was to be expected that infections would occur in the drafty manor. Every room had a fireplace that was constantly lit and tended by a valet. Lady Hawthorne was protected by her mountainous blankets and puffs. She rarely became ill but Thomas was constantly down. His advancing age and corpulence were factors.

Victoria had grown to enjoy having Thomas in her life. He controlled her a great deal, but it was something she deserved. Her affair with the Duke was wrong and it hurt a man that only meant well. She was resigned to live with memories of the man she loved. She would honor her husband until he died and then endure a painful period of mourning. It was how it would be. She would enjoy her husband with all of his negative qualities.

****

"James you have become a very useful servant to me. We began under circumstances that I regret. My pride caused me to take you from Hingham Road. Away from your mother and father. I spoke poorly of your mother but I realize now that I was a jealous old man. Lady Elizabeth and Oliver risked a great deal to preserve their love and you their son. I hope in the end of it all you will understand this old fool." Thomas spoke slowly. He was truly sorry.

"You have given me advantages sir. I will make a great butler someday."

Lord Hawthorne grinned. This young boy had manners the prince himself would envy.

"Have you word of the Duke's life in London?"

"My father is doing as you asked and encouraging his courtship of Lady Madeline. He has made no attempts to contact Lady

Hawthorne. He is not a happy man as he was. He has turned boorish."

"I have apparently succeeded. I do not know why there is little joy in what I have accomplished. That will be all James. Be sure to grab a book as you leave the library."

"I have read them all sir."

"Good bye James." Lord Hawthorne was left alone to his thoughts and a glass of gin.

****

Victoria had spent four days in bed. Her abdominal pain was increasing and the nurse had been called. A surgeon was often not called to birth a child but since he was at the Manor, he had been notified. She had Esther and Liz by her side and a company of other servants. Victoria was calm. The Countess and Lady Elaine were never told Victoria was with child. Thomas gave explanations. He had grown expert at creating believable tales.

Lady Hawthorne gave birth to a boy. The infant was healthy with a full head of golden hair. As all infants, he had blue eyes but Victoria could see a tint of green. The color they would surely become. Victoria was in love. She would teach her son to laugh just as directed by her dying sister.

"You must alert Thomas that he has a son. An heir to the Manor has been born." Lady Hawthorne cried tears of joy. Her tongue caught a drop as it flowed down her cheek. It tasted better than those caused by sorrow did.

There was a crowd at the door waiting to see the baby. Lady Hawthorne was given time to collect herself and the baby was taken away to be cleaned. Victoria held the child in her arms when Lord Hawthorne joined his wife. Her husband had watery eyes. She was not certain if they were tears or lack of sleep.

"My dear Victoria you have given me a son. This old man does not deserve such happiness. He will be a great man. Thank you my lovely wife. We shall name him Edward. Lord Edward Hawthorne."

In silence, Victoria nodded her head in agreement. She thought for a brief moment of Jonathan. He would be proud.

Thomas began shouting orders immediately.

"Esther, pack a bag. You are to help my son grow into a man as wise and delightful as his mother. You shall be in the room next to the nursery."

"Martha I want you to send word to the Earl and Countess and well, everybody."

"Liza. It is your duty to make sure my Lady receives anything she wants."

"I cannot mark a day I have been happier. James I will need you in my study first thing in the morning. I have matters of importance that cannot wait."

There was joy in Derby Manor for the first time since Victoria's arrival. It seemed as nothing could go wrong.

****

"Sir I am here as you asked" James appeared in Lord Hawthorne's study.

"You are if nothing my loyal friend. Do you tire of me James?"

"No Lord Hawthorne. I cannot say I tire of you."

"Do me one favor James. Call me Thomas. It was the name given to me by my father. I do not hear it enough."

"You said you had matters of importance" James hesitated "Thomas"

"Yes James. I have a delivery to be made."

"I will get the courier immediately."

"I have two envelopes to be delivered one year after my death. That should leave enough time for matters to settle themselves. I can say I will be remembered and perhaps revered. I suppose later is better than never."

"I do not follow your reasoning Thomas but I will do as you say"

With that, James disappeared.

****

"Mother is he not the most magnificent child?"

"He is my darling. Good and fat. His eyes are the most beautiful shade of green I have ever seen." Remarked the Countess.

"I agree with you mother he has his father's eyes that is for certain."

"Thomas does not have green eyes Victoria." The countess looked confused.

"Why no he does not, I was referring to the shape of the eyes. They are very round." Victoria was clumsy but she managed to provide an explanation.

"My silly daughter, of course you were referencing the shape. One would otherwise believe Edward is an illegitimate heir." The countess giggled.

"What a joke, there is not a soul within miles that is not hired help. I am married to Lord Hawthorne so of course Edward is the legitimate heir to the Manor. I have a wet nurse. Thomas insisted although I would rather feed my own child. Her name is Jacqueline and she is very agreeable."

"I like Lord Hawthorne's choice to employ a wet nurse. It allowed me freedom to regain my strength quickly to begin work on the next Tompkins child. You were given a wet nurse from the start and then dear Mary, may she rest in peace, came along quickly so the idea worked. I look forward to Edward having a sibling very soon."

"I am blessed with young Edward for now Mother. I have a wet nurse, Liza and of course, Esther, but I enjoy handling the boy myself. I never had…" Victoria abruptly stopped.

"I know of my flaws dear. Society and of course the hope of a large family to fill the Estate had me occupied. I have regrets. After Elaine, I had my troubles and chose society over family. I cannot say it was the correct choice. The Earl is a very patient man and he allowed me to become obsessed with society. I hope within you, you realized my love for you and each of my children." The Countess seemed to be begging Victoria for forgiveness.

"Mother, I know you love me. I am just doing things my own way. Your way was your own."

"Baby Edward is fortunate to have you as a mother. You are very calm in ways that surprise me. I am proud of you Victoria." The Countess was wiping away tears. They were of joy. The type increasingly common within the Manor.

Victoria comforted the fussy child. He was growing to look more as the Duke with each day. Lord Hawthorne made no mention of it. Edward was his son. The manner in which he came into being was never discussed.

Victoria was to visit the stables with Sophie and Hannah that afternoon. The weather was disagreeable in March but Victoria craved the fresh air. She had been indoors for months. She thought of the rides she would regularly take with her sisters at Markham Estate. She longed to return to the White Cliffs of Dover. There was a mystical feeling she got from the place. She made a note in her mind to venture to Dover when the weather improved.

****

"Victoria you must layer on the coats for your outing today. The sky is grey and the winds are fierce. I would say you do not go to the stables today but it is your wish to do so." Esther was preparing Victoria's clothing.

"You know me well Esther. When I have decided to do something, it is done. I do wish to have a short visit with Lord

Hawthorne before my outing. I can go to his study or the drawing room. Wherever he may be."

"The Lord is in the nursery. He has taken a liking to little Edward. He speaks to him as though the boy can make sense of his words. I am not one to tell the Lord how to act around the boy. He is like a father to Edward."

"Hush Esther! Thomas is indeed the father to Edward. I will not have it said any different way. My love affair with the Duke is not to be mentioned in this house. I will not have Edward grow up in the shadows of horrible rumors."

"Yes Lady" Esther bowed out of Victoria's room.

Victoria approached the nursery and found Thomas and Edward both laughing. She did not know her young son could yet giggle and she had never seen Lord Hawthorne in such a casual state. It was so lovely that Victoria quietly stepped away.

****

"Lady Hannah are you prepared to journey to the stables? The weather is not ideal but I believe the freshness of the air can be beneficial."

"I am prepared to brave the elements. Sophie will join us and cook has prepared a basket for us to enjoy."

Sophie, Hannah and Victoria walked the short distance to the stables. They were accompanied by Mavis and James. Victoria was pleased that they were joined by James. She sensed that he came with a story but he was very tight lipped about where he came from or where he was going. Having him on the outing was rare. He seemed to prefer living in the shadows. Still, Victoria found him familiar.

There were at least 16 horses in the stable. There were dapple-greys, chestnuts, black stallions, mares preparing to give birth and a group of Clydesdales. Victoria loved the smells and the walls full of saddles and other gear. She was astonished that she had been nearby such a wonder. It had taken her a long time to discover the treasure.

"Ladies have you never seen a more grand place. Lord Hawthorne and I will encourage Edward to explore these stables. I must come to know these animals. I will pick a favorite to be my own." Victoria was enthusiastic.

"Yes Victoria, it is a worthy spot if you fancy horses. I will say I am delighted to see you so moved." Sophie noted.

"There is a lot which moves me. I am a fortunate to have so many blessings."

"I find myself in a positive disposition as well. Captain Tully has been writing me letters like mad and I believe father is agreeable to a formal courtship this season." Hannah had been aching to share her good news.

"I did not know he was called Captain so soon. You seem to have chosen well Hannah."

"I think we should open the basket and indulge everyone's good fortune."

****

Martha came running from the main house. She was dressed in uniform with no coat waving her arms. She immediately caused concern as her plump body came to the stables.

"My Lady. It is Lord Hawthorne. He was found on the floor of the nursery. The surgeon is with him. Come quickly." Martha was out of breath.

Victoria raced to the house without a word spoken. Her bonnet flew off in the wind as she struggled to be by her husband's side. She had only just seen Thomas as happy as he had ever been. She bounded up the staircase ignoring anyone in her way. It was not the time for social graces.

"Thomas! Please tell me of his condition doctor."

"Lord Hawthorne has suffered an attack of the heart. Without warning, he collapsed. I am afraid his condition is very grave my Lady."

"Victoria" Thomas managed to whisper.

"I am here Thomas. Please do not leave when I need you most. Your son needs you to teach him the ways to be a proper gentleman."

"I am sorry Victoria. I took from you something very dear to your heart. You are a young and beautiful woman. Do not mourn me long. I love you in every way an old man is able."

Lord Thomas Hawthorne closed his eyes.

CHAPTER FIFTEEN

The clocks were stopped at 2:13 in the afternoon. The enormous windows were covered in heavy black velvet coverings and the mirrors were shrouded. Lord Hawthorne's body was embalmed on the property and laid out for visitors in a heavy lead and mahogany casket. The Widow Victoria sat next to the body of her husband for four days and nights. Word had been sent out to alert others of the loss. Visitors came from counties across England to pay their respects.

Victoria was surprised by the readiness of the staff. It was as though they had been expecting the event. Proper mourning attire was already on its way from London and the marble from which to create a monument was waiting. The Widow Victoria had nothing to do but mourn the death of her husband. It was dictated by tradition and custom. Human emotions seemed to be forgotten. It was reasoned that the Queen was the example set for all. She never ceased mourning.

Victoria had a new wardrobe and a new title. It was a great deal of transition for a girl of eighteen years. She had been Lady Victoria, Lady Hawthorne, Dearest Victoria and now she was the Widow Victoria. She would hold the current title for years, perhaps forever in deference to her dead husband.

****

Oliver entered the dining room to find the Duke and his sister enjoying their morning meal. Jonathan had developed a taste for coffee, which he enjoyed with cream and no sugar. Lady Elizabeth was having a bite of meat pie and black tea and cream.

"Good Day Lady Elizabeth, Sir Duke. We received word through courier that there has been a death at Derby Manor in Kent." Oliver announced without obvious reaction.

Jonathan's smile quickly faded and sweat gathered at his temple. He had tried forgetting his love for Victoria but the moment brought her memory to the forefront. He had not mentioned her to Oliver or his sister since the ball at Persimmon House. Lord Hawthorne had warned him that the affair was finished. His words were threatening although he knew not why and he chose to abide by the wishes of the Lord and Lady.

"You have details Oliver?" The Duke showed little emotion.

"It was Lord Hawthorne Sir. Shall I send condolences to the Widow Victoria? You and Lady Elizabeth will surely not be visiting."

"No, I think my sister would agree a note would be appropriate. You handle that for us." The Duke of Wellington replied.

"Do you agree Elizabeth?" He furthered.

"Yes brother. The Widow Victoria must have her privacy at this difficult phase in her life. We only serve as reminders of her past. Certainly, you are otherwise concerned with Lady Madeline. I am so pleased that the Baron has approved of a marriage between you and his daughter."

"It is time that I enter into matrimony and our titles will merge nicely. You realize that it means Madeline will officially become the lady of the house. Will your feelings be bruised? The Duke probed.

"It is expected brother. I am much consumed with my charity endeavors and a busy society schedule."

Oliver looked on at his lovely Elizabeth. His secret and that of James would be buried at Derby Manor. He was required to keep up his portion of the agreement, as Lord Hawthorne surely left this world prepared. The man had a plan for everything.

****

James received the card of condolence from his mother and uncle in London. Either of them did not personally write it. He was pleased that he and his father had successfully kept Jonathan and Victoria apart. He knew of the child but word of the offspring had been kept away from the Duke. She was now the Widow Victoria safely sequestered in the country. The Duke of Wellington was going to marry Lady Madeline. He would keep everyone's secret to protect his mother's name.

James delivered the stack of condolences to Blanche who put them aside for the Widow to look through when time permitted.

"Esther, you have been of great service to me during this stressful time. It was different, but it was love I felt for Lord Hawthorne."

"I am aware Victoria. We are to have the funeral tomorrow and you can begin your official mourning."

"I am going to view the condolence cards left by Blanche. There are many and I will take the time to read them all. I will see you early in the morning to dress for the funeral. I have received dresses and accessories all in black. Edward shall wear a white gown and be shrouded in a black blanket."

Victoria shuffled through the cards until she came upon one from the house of the Duke of Wellington.

Our Sincerest Condolences

Our deepest sympathies in light of Lord Hawthorne's death.

May the peace of God be with you and your loved ones.

The Duke of Wellington and Lady Elizabeth

It was not written in Jonathan's hand. It seemed to be scribbled by Oliver or Lady Elizabeth's secretary. Victoria put the impersonal note back in the pile. She was heart sick, not knowing if it was caused by the death of her husband or the cold note.

****

Esther dressed Victoria in black from head to toe. The fabric was made of bombazine and crepe. She wore a black cameo and onyx earrings. She carried a simple black handkerchief. She led a procession to the gravesite of Lord Hawthorne. It was at the center of the small cemetery surrounded by an iron gate. It was the resting place of a number of his ancestors. He had a massive oblong marble tower to mark his grave ornamented with pewter and gold. Many family and friends were in attendance. The entire day was a blur to Victoria as she was taken over by the loss of her husband and the activities involved in putting him to rest.

Victoria returned to the house to begin her period of seclusion. After all of the guests left the Manor, Victoria climbed the stairs to her room when she came upon James. He slipped by assuring not to engage the widow.

"James, I find you familiar. You are all in black as I have seen before leaving Sherborne in London." Victoria finally realized where she had seen the young man. "I know you to be a very secretive man. I mean you no harm James. I only have one inquiry for you."

"It is not my purpose to deceive you Widow. I was employed as a courier by my last place of employment. I moved up to Lord Hawthorne when the opportunity presented. I may answer a simple question for you. I am a servant only. I doubt I have words to satisfy you." James stood straight and made no reveal of his arrangement.

"James, can you tell me of the Duke of Wellington. I am so removed from society here at the Manor and I will be for some time, I only have curiosity."

James saw an opportunity to make the Widow further forget the Duke.

"I have only come to know through gossip that the Duke of Wellington is to marry Lady Madeline. They are having a party to announce their intentions, shared by the Baron of course. It is all I know Widow Victoria."

"Thank you James. I feel well to have figured out why you are so familiar. I am satisfied now."

Victoria returned to her room after she stopped at the attic staircase where a false step revealed a wooden box. Exhausted, she returned to her bed with memories of the Duke under her arm.

****

Three months of mourning her husband had passed and Victoria made the shocking decision to return to London in time for social season in late June. She was visiting with her sister Lady Elaine in the parlor. It was a small step towards socializing. She was not expected to re-enter society so soon but she would do so with grace and dignity. There would be life beyond the Manor walls for Widow Victoria.

"Elaine, you look well. I do not remember much of the funeral but I know you were present. I appreciate your sympathies. You have so much put upon you in recent years. Your strong will has not gone without notice by Mother and Father. It is now your turn to shine among the Tompkins."

"I appreciate your kind words sister. How is little Edward?"

"He is not yet a year old but he is the sunlight in my life. Since the loss of Thomas, I have felt lonely. The baby cannot avoid making me smile. He is a constant reminder of the goodness of his father." Victoria remarked, unknowing if by "father" she meant Thomas or Jonathan.

"Are you planning to spend the remainder of your formal mourning period here at Derby Manor?"

"I am not Elaine. I should return to Sherborne and enjoy a limited social calendar in London. I feel I have much to contribute to society that I can accomplish as the Widow Victoria. I owe it to Edward to keep the name relevant. He will be respected as Lord Hawthorne as his father was."

"I am to be at Persimmon House with Lady Sterling. Mother and Father will be travelling the continent together. I look forward to viewing their trunks of treasures they acquire on their trip. I will have the staff at Persimmon House to help arrange my social activities and my maid from Markham will be by my side."

"Have you begun filling your calendar?" Victoria asked.

"I am to attend a party thrown by Baron Stephan for the betrothed Lady Madeline and the Duke of Wellington. The Baron and his daughters are intimates so I feel it is my duty to attend. I do not think highly of the Duke due to his reputation and proof seen by my own eyes at the commons. He is a bit of a scoundrel."

"Have you an escort to the party you mentioned?" Victoria cleverly asked.

"I do not as of yet but I have cousins and of course Peter who might act as my escort. We have seen little of Lady Jane. It is assumed that she is with child."

"I would be happy to attend the party with you. It will serve as a perfect event to return to social activities."

"That is a brilliant idea sister. Are you not afraid that people will talk? It represents a rapid mourning period. Gossip gets very sticky."

"I have developed a thick skin Elaine. It is out of necessity and I will hold my head high."

"I will plan for it. You are so brave Victoria."

****

Again, Victoria was faced with change as she prepared to leave for London. She had to see for herself that the Duke had moved on with his life. She had reread every note ever sent by Jonathan. She had thought about every time he touched her or made her laugh and she had dreamed about his green eyes and mischievous smile. She saw Jonathan every day when she cradled her precious Edward. It was time for Victoria to move on with her life.

The trunks were efficiently packed by valets, butlers and footmen. She would leave behind staff to care for the Manor in her absence and since they were no longer needed by Thomas, she left James and James to assure that the house remained standing. Belongings were sent ahead to Nansen Court and with a small caravan, including Esther, Mavis, Blanche, Martha,

Liza and the wet nurse Jacqueline she and Edward headed back to London.

Sherborne was drafty but she enjoyed being back. The early roses were budding and the waterfowl were back on the pond. She noticed the Red Boathouse too and smiled. The new house steward Martin was at the door with several footmen to greet the ladies with cool drinks. They carried in their bags. Edward was happy to be finished with the bumpy ride.

There were coverings on the windows but they were not very black as they were at the Manor. It was time to let a little light back into their lives. It was healthful to everyone's spirits, especially Edward's. Victoria did not want her son raised in an atmosphere of mourning. She thought the Queen might have taken this one a bit too far. Victoria was violating strict codes of custom and conduct by even having such thoughts, but she cared little. She was feeling emboldened by all she had been through.

****

Victoria entered the Baron's home with Elaine and Peter who had decided to join his siblings. She was dressed properly for mourning in black. Her hat showed a small purple detail which was acceptable after several months of black only observance. She did not wear a lot of jewelry except for some black glass earrings.

"My dear Widow Victoria, I have heard you would be in attendance with your close siblings. We consider the Tompkins as part of our family. You have showed kindness to us during a time of loss. If we can do anything to help you in this time of need please inform us? Lord Hawthorne was a fine man, may he rest in peace." The Baron had said all of the right things.

"Thank you Baron. We are here to celebrate the betrothed. It balances the sorrow in our lives."

Victoria, Elaine and Peter shared in condolences showered upon them from those they did not even know. The Widow was waiting for the first glimpse of the betrothed.

Led by Lady Madeline the Duke of Wellington floated across the room towards Victoria and the group gathered around. Lady Madeline spoke first.

"Widow Victoria please accept our most sincere sympathies on the recent loss of you husband, may he rest in peace. I know that the Duke has paid visit to your home and we have known each other for many years. It affected us deeply."

"Lady Madeline speaks on our behalf.

Are you in London for long?

"If you recollect our home is located at Nansen Court where my dear Lord Hawthorne and I received you and Lady Elizabeth."

"I do remember Widow Victoria. If I recall there is a red boathouse adjacent to the main house."

"Your memory is quite precise Duke."

"I forget very little."

Victoria was unable to reply. She was focused on his green eyes and he on her sparling sapphire eyes. No one else in the room existed and no one would guess of the past they shared.

"We must greet our other guests. It is wonderful to see you in such fine form Widow."

Jonathan gave a respectful tip of his grey felt hat and he disappeared.

Victoria stayed at the event until the time was appropriate to leave. She had planned to move on after seeing Jonathan with Lady Madeline but it was hopeless. He still stirred something within her. Victoria's longing for Jonathan had increased over time. He had been cagey but he had seemed happy with his current life. Peter Led the Widow Victoria to the cloakroom to retrieve her belongings. There was a note in her pocket penned on a cloth napkin.

My Victoria,

Your beauty tonight stunned me. I did not know such feelings of desire could strike a man so severely. I am not whole without you. May I intrude upon you one more time? Boathouse when the clock turns midnight.

Yours Forever,

Jonathan

Victoria clutched the scrap to her chest and counted the moments to midnight.

CHAPTER SIXTEEN

Victoria arrived at the boathouse at 11:30. She had not been there since Jonathan said farewell. She never had a chance to say a proper goodbye, as she was not aware that would be their last night together. She brought some cleaning implements since it had been abandoned for over one year. She had a difficult time finding them and it would be a challenge to use them. She had never been required to dust or mop. The fact embarrassed her. She would require Edward to labor, as she believed one never knew when such skills would be required. Why was it good enough for Mavis, while it was considered beneath her? There were no correct answers. She had to be sure to thank the staff for the work they performed. She was so preoccupied by her tasks that midnight came quickly.

Victoria put down her duster to find Jonathan in the doorway.

"I see you have become domestic." He spoke slowly and Victoria cherished every word.

"Only for you."

"Victoria I craved you. It was not only your touch but also the way you move and the look you give me that I know you reserve just for me. You change me Victoria.

"Jonathan I have been on a long journey since we last met. I have been a wife, a widow and…"

Victoria stopped. She was not ready to reveal the truth about Edward. The night was about two people, two bodies, two souls.

Jonathan grabbed the bonnet from her head and released her golden hair. It was not caused to fall out due to childbirth. It had grown softer, longer and it was like fine silk in Jonathan's grasp.

"I am yours tonight Jonathan. No more words."

The bunkroom had been arranged but Jonathan placed her on top of the table where they first made love. The hard surface felt better than the most luxurious bed. Jonathan removed every bit of black from Victoria's body. He kept his eyes fixed on hers. She had forgotten how to feel beautiful. With his body, he brought

Victoria back to life. They fell to sleep on the table. Victoria woke up at dawn.

"Wake my dear. I must get back to the main house." Victoria insisted

"Victoria you do not need to rush away. There are no spies or eyes upon you. Let us enjoy the moment together. I want to see your complexion change as the sun rises. The light's reflection on your hair will bring me tears. Lay with me longer as we enjoy our reunion together.

"Jonathan our situation has not changed. You are about to marry another woman. She is to be your duchess. You still have to explain your despicable behavior as you shared a tryst with Lady Celeste. You were at our flat with her. We are not free to carry on this secret affair. I have to think of Edward." Victoria stopped. She had no control of the words. The truth was out for her explanation.

"Edward? Victoria have you found another man so soon. You are a heartless lady. Lord Hawthorne is barely cold in the ground, you carry on with me and now there is some man named Edward. Is three even enough for you? I need not explain what did or did not happen with Lady Celeste. I trusted your words. I trusted your body. Were you not a virgin on the night we made love on this very surface? Was it some story you created? I know of no man in London society whom to you would be available. He is probably some groom you found at the Manor to fulfill your lust. What say you?"

Victoria was aghast. She had never seen the Duke so angry and confused. He had never been so wrong. He was spitting mad. Victoria became shortly fearful. No person had ever spoken to her this way. He was not a person she was willing to introduce to Edward but now the choice was not hers. She had to reveal the truth.

"Jonathan…"

"I am Sir Jonathan Duke of Wellington. I do not know that I want to hear your lies."

Victoria was trembling. She had barely managed to dress herself. She ran to the door and attempted to escape but in his tirade, Jonathan slammed the door shut.

"I will say the truth Sir Jonathan Duke of Wellington." Victoria managed to compose herself. "This Edward I speak of is but one year old. He is my son. He is your son you fool. It has been my secret. It was my secret shared with only two confidants. One of whom was my husband who gave the boy his last name and title. He saved me from disgrace; He saved Edward from a man like you. You have used your words to belittle me. You doubted me. You will leave this boathouse and never look back Sir."

Victoria ran to the main house. She went to the nursery and scooped up her little cherub.

"I love you Edward. I will raise you to be a proud and mighty man." She kissed young Edward and in return received a smile and a kiss.

****

Victoria returned to her room to find Esther. She closed the door behind her and made certain they were alone. She was so accustomed to being watched, it had become a habit.

"Esther I fear I am going to break into pieces. I saw Jonathan last night at the boathouse and I told him of Edward. I left him speechless. Before I told him, we had a terrible fight. It was a misunderstanding but Esther you should have seen him. He was not the Jonathan I have come to know as a gentle man of respectful words. For so long I have been tortured by my secrets and deception. It has nearly broken me. All I have remaining is Edward. He is my son. He is not anyone else's property. Someday he will not be mine, for I am going to raise him to be an intelligent freethinking man. I will raise him by myself in the country. I will rely heavily on my staff of servants who have become my family.

I shall treat you and the other ladies like you are people not as hired help. I will give you and Liza, Mavis, Blanche, Martha and Jacqueline fine quarters and increased pay. You will have your own library and a tutor. Everyone who works on the manor staff shall learn to read and write. I will keep James and sweet James on hand of course, as I owe them for their loyalty to Lord Hawthorne. Edward and I will create a Manor that all others will envy because it is a place of happy people. I will be a philanthropist, the likes never seen before. I will not be above utilizing a mop on occasion. Maybe I will not go so far as to do that, but my intentions are clear." Victoria stalled to catch a breath.

Esther had thoughts that the Widow had taken leave of her senses.

"My dear peach. You cannot make such grand plans with haste. Jonathan has upset you. You are not of clear mind."

"Jonathan has upset me which is why I must retreat to the country. I will still have Sherborne and London to return to when I wish but I cannot sit by and watch the Duke and Duchess of Wellington live before me. Lady Madeline will provide Jonathan with many children to carry on his name. They will have the freedom to wander about society and London without Edward and me as reminders of the past. I will create a new life among the fields of lavender and horses. I will ride the white cliffs with my boy and tell stories and laugh."

Esther looked into Victoria's eyes and viewed resolve.

"Shall I alert the staff at the Manor to expect our return?"

"Yes Esther."

"My Lady are you going to allow Sir Duke to see his son before we depart." Esther gently asked.

"No. He cannot see Edward. Jonathan is my past and Edward is my future. The two shall not mingle."

****

The Duke returned to his home to find Elizabeth in the dining room finishing her breakfast. He hurried past Oliver without a word. He closed the door behind him, which was not usually his custom.

"Jonathan, Hello. Did you sleep late? Too much gaiety at the party last night? You do look a bit out of sorts brother. Is there something the matter?" Elizabeth questioned Jonathan.

"Elizabeth, the words I am to speak are ours alone."

Elizabeth was concerned. "Of course you may speak freely".

"I saw Victoria last night. We spent the night together once more and it was enchanting. The sun rose and we had a terrible misunderstanding. I released words that I regret. I caused Victoria to shudder in fear. My Victoria was victim of my vitriol."

"She left me without words. I wanted to follow her as she ran back into the main house. I let her go be with Edward." Jonathan paused.

"Your words confuse me." Elizabeth was fixated.

"Edward is her boy. I am a father."

The Duke left the dining room. His comment left Elizabeth bewildered.

****

"We leave for Derby Manor today dear boy. I am sorry you have to endure another bumpy carriage ride so soon. We are to make our home in the country where you will ride great horses and read tales and poetry. One day you will fall in love with a smart woman of your own choosing. Wait for true love my sweet Edward. I am one who knows it exists." Edward just smiled.

With Sherborne almost behind her, Victoria walked the grounds. It was the home to a great love. It is where a 17-year-old girl became a woman. It was time for Victoria to take the reins of her life and turn the carriage straight. She was soon to embark on a path not often travelled. She would have to create new grooves in the dirt on which she would travel upon.

Victoria stopped to smell a dainty pink rose.

She left for the country.

****

A note arrived for Victoria the next day.

Victoria,

I have embarrassed myself with negligence. A human life born of our love is testament to our enduring bond. You must let me into a life, which is ours to share. I do not take another breath without you and our son. May I intrude on your life one more time? There shall be no exit. I plead.

Jonathan

It was returned unopened. Jonathan was told Widow Victoria was gone.

****

Jonathan was hopeless. He considered his life in society with Madeline by his side. He would enjoy his title and endless monetary benefits. Victoria and the threat of discovery that he had an illegitimate child would disappear. Jonathan penned another note.

Baron Stephan,

May I intrude upon your parlor today at 3pm? It is a matter of urgency and discretion will be necessary. Faithfully, your friend.

Sir Jonathan, Duke of Wellington

He sent it through courier with instructions to wait for reply.

****

The Duke sat across from Baron Stephan in his parlor. He had been a widower for many years and the lack of feminine touch was evident. His daughters were busy in their own pursuits. Their efforts were evident but the Baron's taste prevailed.

"I was surprised to receive your message with such urgency Duke. I imagine it concerns my daughter Madeline and the contract of marriage. It is a pity that financial contracts and details must surround a joyous event."

"Baron I come to you out of respect for you and your family name. Most importantly, out of the honor and respect I have for Lady Madeline."

The Baron interrupted.

"We do not have to speak of your reputation. Your lifestyle and long list of conquests are on the mouths of many. I have been a young man myself, long before the blissful years spent with my dearly departed wife. I believe you to be reformed thus a suitable match for my daughter. I in fact believe that honor and respect will lead to love. I consider the matter settled. You and Lady Madeline are betrothed. You presented as a couple to society just two nights ago. I think all is said Duke. Am I not correct?"

Jonathan spoke.

"You are sadly not correct Baron Stephan. I must end my plans to wed your daughter. I have found myself very improperly but desperately devoted to another. She has borne me a son out of marriage. Secrets have been a plague and they must stop before lives that are more innocent are shattered. I am ready to accept my shame. I wish not to harm Lady Madeline. She will not be brought into my web of deceit. Forgive me Baron."

The Duke of Wellington was overcome by emotion. He showed tears to another man for the first time in his adult life.

"Duke of Wellington, you have brought scandal into my home. Your title means dirt in this city. You are worse than the bon vivant you are rumored to be. I will explain all to my lovely daughter. You are never to contact Madeline through courier or personal appearance. Her reputation will be saved. Yours will be destroyed. Say farewell to London society as you once knew it."

"I take my shame. Please consider my gentle sister Lady Elizabeth. She was but a bystander in my deceptive life."

"I have no words for your sister. She will be spoken of an old spinster with money whose family failed her. I do not see her social calendar filling in short time."

"Thank you Baron,"

Jonathan departed with his felt hat crushed in his palms when the Baron spoke.

"As a man Jonathan I must speak from my own broken heart. If a son of yours is to live a life free of lies and scandal, you must go to him. Claim she, whom you claim devotion towards and your boy. I have known love and if you are lucky enough to find it you are a blessed man."

Jonathan left and he felt relieved. He was free. The Duke rushed home to share his plans with Elizabeth.

CHAPTER SEVENTEEN

Jonathan rode through London on horseback towards his home for one of the final times. His hat was left on the steps of Baron Stephan's house. His hair blew in the breeze and he ripped off his satin bowtie. He felt as though he had just shed pounds from his frame. He was a free man. There were no more walls standing between him and Victoria. He had obstacles to conquer but those details were minor. His goal was in clear sight.

Jonathan corrected his route and turned towards Sherborne at Nansen Court. Explaining all to Elizabeth could wait. Victoria was now his priority and his son, Edward.

At first sight, he viewed a crew of laborers on the far end of the pond. They were not working on the red boathouse. They were dismantling the structure. It was being taken down board by board. The site was his first stop.

"Stop your work! What is it you are doing to my boathouse?" Jonathan approached the foreman.

"I am sorry Sir. I am following the detailed instructions of the Widow. We have been ordered to take the structure down piece by piece and after we are to set fire to the foundation. Next spring, the land will recover and a garden is to be planted."

"I am the Duke of Wellington and I order a stop to your work. You will be paid handsomely for your trouble." Jonathan insisted.

"The Widow left warning of your possible visit. We are to continue. The Widow has already paid us handsomely Sir and as the property owner with her son Lord Edward Hawthorne, they have rights to their property. I think a garden of roses will be lovely"

"I have been put in my place. I am sorry to have disturbed your work."

Jonathan continued to the house where he would demand to see Victoria. She could avoid his letters but she would not deny his visit. He used the heavy rosette knocker and a strange face appeared.

"Yes Sir, May I be of help?"

"I am the Duke of Wellington and I am here to visit the Widow Victoria."

"I am honored by you presence Duke, but the Widow has left Sherborne. She did not leave word of where she went or if she might return."

"Has she left note for me, "Jonathan"?"

"No Duke. I am new to Sherborne but there was no word left for you. Her departure was sudden."

"Thank you." Jonathan continued on to share word with his sister. He rode home slowly.

****

The carriage came to a halt when it arrived at Derby Manor. Victoria breathed a sigh of relief. She and Edward were home. The staff arrived in carriages behind hers and some were already present to welcome the Widow and Lord Edward.

"Jacqueline, please take Edward to his nursery. Do you know if it has been decorated per my instructions?"

"Yes Widow. The colors are bright and the rocking horse has been brought from Markham Estate."

"I will visit later. Make certain that Edward is comfortable in his surroundings. I will have a meal and visit Edward before I retire to my room."

"As you wish Widow. May I speak?"

"Yes Jacqueline"

"On behalf of the house staff we wish to welcome you back to the Manor. We will do all to make it a comfortable setting for you and Lord Edward."

"My thanks to you and all of the staff. There will be many changes afoot. Our highest priority is Edward. You may take him now."

Jacqueline left with Edward. James had been summoned to the foyer. He appeared immediately.

"James you cannot hide your intelligence from me. I have seen you reading books that Lord Hawthorne collected and never read. Please share your love of knowledge with Edward. I want him to develop a curiosity for life as you have. You are still a mystery to me but I shall leave you to your privacy. Whoever had a hand in your upbringing saw great things in you."

"Thank you widow Victoria. I am honored to serve you and young Edward."

Victoria ate some bread and fresh cheese for dinner. She had an appetite for little else. After her meal, she went to sleep in her sumptuous bed where she slept deeply.

****

Jonathan joined Elizabeth for breakfast in London. He ate a small portion of toast with marmalade, for he had appetite for little else.

"Elizabeth, I have told all to the Baron. Madeline and I are no longer to be married. Word will spread rapidly. I hope that your good name will avoid the approaching inferno. It is not to be pleasant. I have confessed my inappropriate my devotion to another. I have claimed responsibility for a son born of my affair. I will lose my title and good standing. I have financial means but nothing compared to what I have lost."

Elizabeth stopped Jonathan.

"My dear brother it is just a name. Sacrifices have been made for namesake that have caused grave suffering." Elizabeth held her words. It was not the time to share her secret life with James and Oliver. "What of the Widow Victoria and the boy. The boy that is your son?"

"Victoria has left Sherborne with Lord Edward and no plans to return. Her name will soon be revealed. It is only a matter of time. I must find her and tell that her name in London will be tarnished. She and Edward will recover from the shame. I have made a mess." Jonathan sat with head in hand.

"I know of Victoria's retreat to Derby Manor. I know that she and Edward are well. He is just beginning to walk and he has brilliant green eyes like those of his father. I am apprised of what she eats every day. She smiles and she smells of lily of the valley. She reads each night in her library upon a red satin chaise. Elizabeth, you will be happy to hear that she favors the head steward by the name of James. He is bold and intelligent. He does not carry himself as a hired man." Oliver finished.

"You have seen my Victoria?"

"Not with my own eyes. Go to her."

****

"Good morning Widow. I have word that Lady Elaine is planning a visit from Markham today. She is spending some time their waiting for your parents return. She would like to visit the stables with you. She asked that you dress appropriately for a short ride."

"It sounds like great fun. I will have Esther prepare the proper riding attire. I will have a visit with Edward before I meet my sister in the foyer. Have cook prepare a basket."

"Of course Lady Victoria,"

Victoria was pleased by Blanche's slip of the tongue. She preferred being call Lady rather than Widow. She still observed mourning in many ways but she knew Thomas would prefer she move forward with her moniker. She was delighted to see Elaine and have the opportunity to become acquainted with the horses.

"Hello Elaine! I am so pleased you have come for a visit. I long to hear about the season in London after my departure" Victoria welcomed Elaine

"I do not have much news. I have spent the last months at the Estate. I had a lot of thinking to do. Having done that I am ready to visit my sister in the country side."

They began their walk to the stables. It was a sunny fall day. Victoria noticed a maturity in young Elaine. Her baby sister was becoming a beautiful young woman.

"Elaine, you must tell me his name. You have a secret you are keeping. Is he with you at Markham? Is it a proper match? Do give me his name."

"Sister, you think you know everything. The name is Gray." Elaine stated coyly.

"I know how to keep a secret my sister. The walls of the Manor are the only ones listening to me. This is great news. Tell me of this Gray?"

"It is not a name of a man, but of a book. I am studying "Gray's Anatomy". It is a recent publication about the human body. I am to study medicine in Bath, beginning next year. I have yet to tell mother and father. I want to heal people sister. I love life in high society but my aspirations are grander." Elaine glanced at Victoria for reaction.

"My sister the doctor. I am so proud of you Elaine. Mother and father will be as well. It may take mother time to shine to the idea, but she will." Victoria threw her arms around Elaine.

"I was worried to tell you. I feared you would be disappointed. Victoria I have brought you a surprise from Markham. I can see that your disposition is not in need of rescue but I made the arrangement.

The ladies entered the Stables to find the groom preparing the horses for their ride.

"Hello old friend!"

"Benjamin"

Elaine had brought the horseman from the Estate as a token of the past and hope for the future.

"I am so happy to see you at the Manor."

"Victoria, Benjamin is here to stay. Arrangements have been made for him to be in charge of your stables. There is no one left at the Estate to ride. Soon Edward will be in the saddle. I thought Benjamin would be an appropriate trainer."

"Elaine, your gift is perfect. Benjamin we will move to move your entire family over. Your wife will not work in the laundry. She will be treated with respect and free to cook and raise her children in peace."

"It will be our new home."

"Welcome home Benjamin."

****

With only Victoria on his mind, Jonathan packed a few trunks and travelled through the night to Derby Manor. He did not know from whom Oliver got his information. He cared little about details. He longed to hold Victoria in his arms. He would not let her go this time.

When Jonathan pulled near Derby Manor, he felt a chill run through his body. Perhaps his feelings were not proper but they could no longer be concealed.

Jonathan's knock alerted James to answer the door. Victoria was in the library on her red chaise sipping Chamomile tea before bedtime.

"May I help you Sir." James asked softly.

"My name is Jonathan Forsythe and I am here, unannounced, to see Lady Victoria."

Victoria came out of the library. She was bewildered.

"Jonathan." She was breathless. "What are you doing here and who is Forsythe?"

"It is the last name given to me by my father. I have given up my title and my entire life. Victoria I do not care to be the Duke of Wellington. I am Jonathan Forsythe and I love you Victoria."

"I love you Jonathan, or whatever you call yourself. We do not need titles for happiness you fool. We only need each other and our son. Jacqueline! Come at once and bring Lord Edward."

The staff had been listening and through their tears of joy. They already had Edward down the staircase.

"Jonathan meet your son Edward"

"It is a year past the day Thomas died. He asked that I give this letter to you Victoria and this one to you James"

"James I appreciate your loyalty to Lord Hawthorne but you must let us enjoy the moment" Victoria pleaded.

Jonathan spoke up. "Read the letter and this James is cousin to my butler Oliver. Perhaps the letter will make sense of the mess."

"James Explain your letter" Jonathan asked.

"I am given conservatorship of Derby Manor along with Lady Victoria until Lord Edward turns of age. Living under the roof with me are to be my parents Lady Elizabeth Forsythe and Oliver Marlow."

Jonathan stood with his mouth agape. "You are my nephew? Oliver and my sister all of these years?"

"Jonathan we will have time for details later. Lord Thomas Hawthorne invites you to your new home at Derby Manor with your son Edward who inherits the Lordship.

Jonathan and Victoria embraced.

Made in the USA
Lexington, KY
28 October 2013